GAY DEFEAT

Disarmingly lovely, Delia Beringham is the only daughter of a wealthy financier who indulges her every whim. It is Delia's hope that her lover, Lionel Hewes, will leave his wife for her — but the sudden crash of the Beringham family fortune and her father's suicide change all that. Lionel abruptly fades from the picture, and Delia is left with only her own courage and determination to sustain her. So what is she to say when her father's friend, Martin Revell, chivalrously offers her his hand in marriage?

DENISE ROBINS

GAY DEFEAT

Complete and Unabridged

LINFORD
Leicester

First published in Great Britain in 1933

First Linford Edition
published 2020

A catalogue record for this book is available
from the British Library.

ISBN 978–1–4448–4487–0

Published by
Ulverscroft Limited
Anstey, Leicestershire

Set by Words & Graphics Ltd.
Anstey, Leicestershire
Printed and bound in Great Britain by
T. J. International Ltd., Padstow, Cornwall

This book is printed on acid-free paper

1

When Delia walked through the beautiful, cool lounge of the Ritz at cocktail time that bright August morning, people looked at her and then turned to look again.

The tall, fair man who followed her through the lounge, and seated himself beside her at one of the small tables, had more than admiration in his gaze when he looked at her.

'What will you have, my sweet?'

'A gin and It, I think,' she said. 'It's frightfully hot. I do hate London in August; it's unbearable, isn't it, Lingo?'

Lionel Hewes, known to his particular circle of friends as 'Lingo', drew a thin gold cigarette-case from his pocket and handed it to the girl.

'I'd hate it if *you* weren't in town.'

That drew a smile and a sigh from her. She rejected the cigarette, shaking her head, and peeled off her long, delicate suede gloves. Then she took a little gilt and enamel box from a green silk bag, which had her monogram D in diamonds, and examined her face in the mirror. Delia, at twenty, had no need to resort to cosmetics. Dark eyes, rather almond-shaped, thickly lashed, which flashed like onyx when she laughed; hair, black and sleek as a raven's wing, cut straight; and this was Delia. She did not look altogether English. Her mother had been French. But she had been born and bred in London and was the finished, expensive product of her day.

The French mother had died when Delia was ten. Her father, Charles Beringham, had brought up this one and only daughter in the way which he considered best. He was a very rich and a very busy man. He adored Delia and saw as much of her as he could. She had had luxury and attention since she was born, and because she was exceedingly pretty and amusing she had also had more than her fair share of flattery and spoiling. If her mind was given up largely to the pursuit of pleasure, it was not to be wondered at. She had had nothing else to think about, until early this summer. Then she had met Lingo Hewes. She had fallen in love with him, and she found that being in love gave her a great deal too much to think about. Especially when the affair was as difficult as it was disturbing.

Lingo was a married man. Delia had tried hard not to fall in love with him, but she was not really given a fair chance. He was ten years older than she was and extremely attractive. Very expert at lovemaking and flattery was Lingo; a little too expert, perhaps. But Delia thought him marvellous, and it was rather thrilling to have this secret affair. At least it was a secret from her father, if from nobody else, in their circle of mutual friends. And they were quite certain that it was a secret from Lingo's wife.

This morning, sitting in the Ritz with

Lingo, Delia felt a little less gay and hopeful than usual. She raised her cocktail, looked at the ice-cold pallid liquid which gleamed through the misted glass, and said sadly:

'How's it all going to end, Lingo?'

'It can only end one way,' he said, and stretched out his long legs and drew deeply on his cigarette, watching Delia through the blue smoke. 'We must chuck everything and go.'

'Darling, I think I would, if I hadn't got such a conscience. But there's your wife and my father.'

'My wife,' said Lingo coldly, 'won't suffer much if we do quit. She isn't in love with me any more. We've been married six years, and for the last two we've lived in the same house like strangers. Phil will be perfectly satisfied with her freedom and alimony.'

'The thought of Daddy is a great worry,' announced Delia, while she sipped her drink. 'He adores me, and I think it would be an awful blow to him if you and I eloped, Lingo darling.'

'But he'd soon forgive you — he doesn't dislike me.'

'Nobody could dislike you, darling,' said Delia, with one of her sweet, flashing smiles. 'But I think Daddy might feel less friendly towards you, if he knew how it was with you and me.'

'I've been awfully good, my sweet.'

'Frightfully,' she agreed. 'We've both been good.'

'But it can't go on. I want you to belong to me — for ever.'

'Do you really love me as much as that?' she whispered.

His hand reached out for hers. Swiftly he kissed the shell-pink polished tips of the slender fingers.

'You know it, Angel.'

Her heart beat a shade faster.

'If only you were free!' she sighed.

'I must get my freedom, that's all.'

'And then there's Martin Revell,' added Delia.

The man beside her frowned. A slight colour ran up under his fair skin, which showed that he was irritated. The mere name of Revell was sufficient to irritate him. Damn the man — he played much too prominent a part in Delia's existence. He was always at the Beringhams' house; Charles Beringham made an absurd fuss of him. Martin's father had been the Beringhams' solicitor for years. And now that he was dead, young Revell was carrying on his father's business and seemed to have made himself very popular with the famous financier. But that seemed to Lingo no reason for foisting himself upon Delia at the same time.

'There's Martin!' repeated Delia. 'Daddy's always urging me to be nice to him.'

'Why should you?'

'I must say I'm not interested in him. I'm in love with you.'

'But you wouldn't have looked at young Revell anyhow, even if you hadn't met me, would you?'

'No, I don't think I should. But there has never been any question of love between us.'

She spoke emphatically.

'Don't let us think about Martin,' she said, after a pause. 'Let's think of ourselves and what we're going to do.'

'That's certainly more to the point,' said Lingo, and looked at her through narrowed lids.

'Look here, darling,' he said, leaning a little nearer her, 'supposing we take the plunge tonight?'

She looked at him, startled.

'What do you mean?'

'I mean, supposing we face your father together and tell him that we love each other and that I'm going to get a divorce and marry you.'

'Oh, Lingo — do you think we dare — ?'

'Don't you love me enough?'

'I feel so guilty about your wife.'

'You needn't. She won't mind divorcing me.'

Delia's bright eyes turned away from him a moment.

'Let's have some lunch here and talk it over,' suggested the man.

'I'd love that,' she said.

'I'll see the head waiter and order something special for you. You love red roses — you shall have some on your table.'

He spoke eagerly. He felt that this lunch was going to be the deciding factor in their lives. He left her for a moment and she followed the tall, smart figure with her gaze, and thought how marvellous he was to her; sweet to think of the red roses.

She might have had a little shock if she could have overheard the conversation between Lingo Hewes and another man of his own breed whom he met in the bar at this precise moment.

'Can you lend me a tenner, old boy? I've got to take a girl out to lunch and I'm broke.'

The man in question lent Lingo the tenner and passed on, wondering whom he could sting for twenty pounds at the club, as he was himself by way of being broke.

Lingo Hewes gave Delia her lunch

and made himself more than usually attractive during the meal. The result was a success. Delia said:

'I'm going to be all brave, darling, and we'll put it to Daddy this evening. He's sure to help me.'

'I hope to God he does,' said Lingo devoutly.

They walked out of the hotel into a brilliant blaze of sunshine. Piccadilly felt and looked swelteringly hot. Delia gasped as she drew on her gloves.

'Let's walk — you can come with me as far as home, can't you?'

'What are you doing this afternoon?' Lingo asked, as he fell into step beside her, going towards Charles Street, where the Beringhams had lived for the last fifteen years.

'I've got my friend, Betty Willis, who was in Paris with me, coming to tea.'

'Lucky Betty — ' began Lingo, and then stopped. His attention had become arrested by the headlines of a poster held by a newspaper man at the corner of the street. 'Hallo,' he added, 'what's this?'

Delia followed his gaze.

'What's what?'

'See what that poster says.'

Delia read it. The headlines flamed at her:

SUDDEN CRASH OF WELL-KNOWN
FINANCIER FOLLOWED BY SUICIDE

Delia's heart gave a little jerk.

'Lord, how horrid! I wonder if it's one of Daddy's friends. Buy a paper, Lingo, and see.'

They stopped in front of a newspaper man and Lingo bought the *Evening Special*. Walking slowly along beside Delia, he unfolded the paper. Then he stopped dead.

'Good God!' he exclaimed, and the colour mounted to his forehead.

'What's the matter, Lingo?'

She had never seen him so perturbed. She reached out her fingers for the paper. He tried to fold it up and keep it away from her, but she snatched it from him. A horrible fear had sprung to life within her.

'No — let me see — don't stop me, Lingo.'

Then she saw the name leaping at her from the evening paper:

'CHARLES BERINGHAM. *Beringham, the well-known financier, found dead in his office, with a revolver in his hand. Suicide following news of his ruin . . .* '

The paper dropped from Delia's hand on to the pavement.

'Oh!' she said in a moaning voice. 'Oh, Daddy — *Daddy!*'

Lingo Hewes put an arm around the slim, young figure. He thought that she was going to faint. In a panic, he hurried her to the kerb, hailed a passing taxi, put her in it, and gave the driver her home address. Then he took his place beside her. His face was almost as pale as hers. And he was thinking:

'My God, what a frightful blow — not only for her — but for *me*!'

★ ★ ★

In the library of Beringham's house in Charles Street, Martin Revell stood before the open window, watching every taxi or private car that rolled down the street. He was watching for Delia to come home.

Martin had just returned here from the mortuary. He had identified Charles Beringham's remains, and come away sick at heart, realising that not only had he lost a valuable client, but a cherished friend.

A taxi drew up at the door, and Martin Revell hastened out to meet it. Then he caught a glimpse of Delia's white little face and stricken eyes, and hurried to her side, stirred with love and pity for her.

'Delia — you poor child — so you know — !'

She allowed him to take her arm and

12

lead her into the house.

In the cool green library Delia sank into the chair before her father's desk and pulled off the impudent little cap, which looked so incongruous now that the colour and brilliance had been wiped from her face.

She stared dully up at Martin Revell, who had been her father's friend.

'Tell me everything,' she said, and shielded her eyes with her hand.

He told her a little, but not all. She was shaken to the core as she listened to the quiet, deep voice of the man, and realised that while she had been drinking cocktails and dancing and dining, her father had been floundering in waters too deep for him to swim — drowning — lonely and alone.

'If only I'd known!' she whispered.

'What could you have done?' he said gravely.

The dark, silky head shot up. Delia looked at him with blazing eyes.

'Of course — you don't think I'm fit to do anything helpful, do you?'

Her expression, and the rough note in her voice, startled him.

'Why, Delia — '

'Oh, I know you despise me!' she broke in. 'You've always looked upon me and my friends as being useless members of society! I know that well enough!'

Martin Revell flushed to the roots of his hair.

'Don't let's quarrel just now, please,' he said huskily.

She caught her breath on a sob — or a laugh — it might have been either.

'Give me a cigarette,' she said.

It was the old Delia speaking. She needed a cigarette — something to hide the fact that she was frightened and unhappy.

He gave her a cigarette, got up and began to pace the library.

'Tell me,' she said, 'will this mean that I shan't have a penny — literally?'

He paused in front of her, running his thin, nervous fingers through hair which was dark, prematurely greying over the ears.

'I'm afraid so,' he answered her.

'Not a single penny!'

'It's early days to say anything definite, but I don't think there will be anything left, Delia. His liabilities are enormous — that last gamble went wrong — and he just couldn't face it, that's all.'

She winced and turned away from him.

'How frightful.'

He looked at the dark, pretty head. His heart was hammering as it had never done in his life before.

'Delia — my poor child — '

'I shall be all right,' she broke in, with a gesture of irritation, as though his pity jarred her nerves. 'You needn't worry. I can't quite realise it yet — it's hard to believe that my home — everything will go. But I can work, I suppose, and I know someone, anyhow, who will stick to me.'

She was thinking of Lingo — Lingo, who was madly in love with her and wanted to leave his wife for her sake.

She felt quite sure that she could go to him and that he would take care of her.

'You know that I will always stick to you, Delia. I loved your father. He was my friend. I served him until he died, and now I only ask to serve you.'

She looked up at him and then looked away again quickly, embarrassed.

'Sweet of you, Martin.'

'Not at all. This is hardly the time — ' He was stammering like a boy, his eyes burning, his fingers shaking: 'But if you'll do me the honour — I mean, if you'd marry me — I'll take care of you for the rest of your life.'

She sat still, staring up at him, then the bright pink rushed to her cheeks. She gave a nervous laugh.

'My dear Martin — are you proposing to me?'

'Yes,' he said bluntly.

Delia took her cigarette from the ash-tray and drew deeply on it. Her cheeks were still bright and her eyes brilliant. But she was raw with pride and nerves, and she thought:

'He's sorry for me — just because I'm down and out. He doesn't really care a button for me that way.'

Aloud, she said:

'I'm grateful, Martin. Thanks — awfully! But I wouldn't dream of accepting your kind offer. As a matter of fact, I'm going to marry somebody else.'

He stood still, his body stiffening.

'May I ask who?'

'Lingo Hewes — as soon as he can get his divorce.'

Martin Revell stared blankly down at Delia's defiant young face.

'Good God!' he exclaimed.

Delia's lashes fluttered and drooped.

'I don't see why you should say that. There are thousands of divorces every day, and if Lingo and I really love each other — '

'Delia — for God's sake think seriously before you do it.'

'I've already thought — '

'And what about Mrs. Hewes?'

Delia's dark, silky brows drew together in a frown.

'I'm awfully sorry about her. That's the one thing against it. But Lingo says she won't mind — she wants to be free.'

'Very well. And can he afford to support two wives in comfort?'

'*Two* wives! That sounds rather beastly.'

'It's no good glossing over facts, Delia.'

'We haven't actually discussed what he can afford,' she admitted. 'I hate talking about money, but I'm quite sure that Lingo can look after me. He's said so, dozens of times. He has a private income, you know.'

Martin, with a feeling of hopelessness, walked to the window and stared blindly out of it.

'Delia — let's be friends. I want to help you — and if Hewes really cares about you and means to marry you — well, I might be able to do something there.'

That was sporting of him, she

thought, decent. He could be a dear when he wanted. Tears rushed to her eyes.

'All right. I don't want to quarrel with you. You've been very good to me. And it's sweet of you to bother about me, but wasn't it a little too quixotic of you to ask me to marry you just because of what's happened?'

His heart leapt to his throat. He caught her hand and said:

'But it wasn't altogether that — '

He broke off, dismayed. She had burst into tears.

Martin tried to comfort her, quieten her, but she went on crying. Her grief for her father was, at least, genuine, and it had momentarily broken her.

* * *

Delia Beringham ceased abruptly to dance her way through life.

During the week that followed her father's sudden and violent end, she realised that she had reached a grave crisis in her particular existence.

Martin came frequently to the house, and was with Delia as much as possible, dividing his time between the ordinary routine of work and the especial attention which he was giving the affairs of the late Charles Beringham.

She spent the day, after she had learned the tragic news, in bed, refusing to see anybody. But the telephone rang repeatedly, and she answered her special friends, lying on her pillows, the instrument in her hand, feeling sick with too much crying.

Dozens of her friends were swift to sympathise. Everybody had seen the news in the evening papers. They all said:

'So *frightfully* sorry, darling . . . what on earth will happen to you?'

Lady Berrell sent carnations and a note:

'*Too* ghastly, my dear. Let me come round in the morning . . . '

One after the other they telephoned, full of pity and curiosity. And if curiosity was the dominating factor with most of them, Delia did not realise it. She thought of what Martin had said about her friends 'falling off', once they knew her position. She told herself that he would have to take that back when he saw how they were rallying round her.

Certainly they came, bevies of them — smartly dressed men and women, pouring into the house in Charles Street at all hours of the day, with flowers and inquiries. Martin Revell watched them come and go and said nothing. But he was not deceived. He knew that they flocked to Delia in a fever of excitement, of morbid curiosity, which would come to a rapid end.

Perhaps, of them all, Martin found Betty Willis the most genuine. She was a lazy, thoughtless, attractive girl of Delia's own age, with a genius for dress and nothing much else. But she was devoted to Delia — he did not think she would fail when the others had vanished. She came at once, with a suitcase, to stay in the house with Delia so that she should not sleep there alone.

And of course Lingo Hewes called, two or three times a day. If there ever a man on earth Martin disliked and distrusted, it was Lingo. But Delia wanted him, and Martin stood aside.

Martin persuaded her not to go to the funeral, and on that melancholy morning, Lingo came and sat with her in the charming room decorated in green velvet and silver-leaf, which was her own sitting-room. He held her in his arms and kissed and comforted her, when she collapsed in tears, sick with horror at the thought of what was taking place at the crematorium.

'Something rather beastly happened yesterday,' Delia told Lingo, when she stopped crying and could talk to him calmly. 'Marie telephoned to Pacquille, where I've had an account for months, and tried to get some black dresses, and they were positively rude to her. They said it must be cash or nothing.'

Lingo raised his brows but went on

stroking Delia's slender hand.

'What a damned shame, darling,' he murmured.

He did not quite like the significance of what Delia told him. Of course, Pacquille were afraid they wouldn't get their money. The cat was out of the bag about Beringham.

It was tough on Delia. Lingo knew perfectly well she wasn't going to get a penny. A frightful blow for the poor little thing; just when she was beginning to enjoy life, and so adorably pretty and attractive. He was stirred to passion for her, this morning, even when those bright, dark eyes of hers were dimmed by crying. She was far and away the most fascinating girl he had ever known and loved. He dropped a kiss into the palm of her hand.

'I hate to see you look so sad, my sweet.'

She gave him a touching smile.

'I don't know what I would have done without you, Lingo. Betty's been a dear — but it's you who have saved me from going out of my mind with worry.'

'I've done nothing,' he said modestly, 'it's just driven me crazy only being able to see you in snatches — Phil's been so trying — asking a lot of questions about you. And I'm jealous of that fellow, Revell, always in the house.'

'You needn't be jealous of Martin. He's poor Daddy's executor — so naturally he's here a lot. I must say he's been frightfully decent to me — he's a funny, serious old thing, but he's a good friend.'

'Ah, but you need more than that, you poor darling,' said Lingo, and stroked her arm with a regular soothing movement.

'I couldn't have borne losing Daddy in that terrible way, if I hadn't had you,' Delia whispered. She spoke in all sincerity, genuinely thankful for Lingo and his love. 'It's all been so awful! My friends have been kind, but it's you who really matter.'

'Sweet thing,' repeated Lingo and thought uneasily of a little paragraph in this morning's paper which had said that even Beringham's life insurance had been borrowed from up to the hilt; that all his properties would have to be sold up to meet his liabilities.

'I can't quite think what's going to happen,' said Delia, and put a hand to her forehead in a bewildered fashion. 'Martin said last night that poor old Daddy had gambled away his last halfpenny. All this' she indicated the boudoir — 'will have to go. Everything. I shall be left with nothing — except one or two jewels and my clothes. I suppose they can't take those away from me.'

'We won't let them, darling,' said Lingo gallantly.

'By the way, Martin said that most of my friends would vanish, once they knew my position,' went on Delia.

'Cheerful fellow,' said Lingo. 'I really cannot stand Revell at any price.'

Delia, with a sense of loyalty, made haste to say:

'He's really awfully nice — but he has

a blunt way of putting things. It's what he thinks — he can't help it. And Lingo, I told him about — us.'

'Was that quite wise, darling?'

'He had to know some time.'

'What did you tell him?'

'That we love each other and that you would marry me as soon as you got your divorce.'

Lingo busied himself lighting a cigarette.

'And what did he say to that?'

'Oh — he wasn't particularly pleased — I don't suppose one could expect him to be. Martin's like one of the family and of course he feels a certain amount of responsibility for me now that Daddy's gone. But I told him he needn't worry — you'd look after me.'

'Darling!' said Lingo, but his brain was working overtime, circling round the thought of finance rather than Delia's personal welfare.

Delia lay back on her cushions and closed her eyes. She was remembering Martin's proposal of marriage. Of course she could not tell Lingo about that — it wouldn't be fair to poor old Martin.

Suddenly she opened her eyes and regarded Lingo anxiously.

'Did you say just now that your wife was asking questions about me?'

'H'm — yes. A bit on the raw at the moment because Connie Berrell saw us lunching at the Ritz that day we heard the bad news, and told her. I really ought to have met Phil for lunch that morning.'

Delia sat upright, nervously pulling at the square of black chiffon which she called a handkerchief. Her cheeks were red. She did so hate the thought that Lingo was married. She said in a low tone:

'It worries me, Lingo, to think I'm taking you away from another woman. Of course you ought to have kept your lunch appointment. But you've always assured me that she — she doesn't care for you any more.'

'She doesn't. It was all pique. She

was annoyed because you're so much younger and prettier, perhaps, and that made her inquisitive.'

It was a caddish remark but it passed by Delia, who was so worried and so blindly in love.

'Lingo,' said Delia, in an earnest voice, 'I'm trying so hard to pull myself together and think about the future. Lingo, what *are* we going to do?'

He had guessed that was coming. He squared his shoulders to face it.

'We'll think it out — but don't trouble your pretty head today — you've got so much to face. Forget it — in my arms.'

'Yes, think it all out and tell me what we can do,' she whispered, curving an arm about his neck. 'The best thing will be to do what you said at the Ritz that day — go through with the divorce at once. You are sure that *she* wants a divorce, aren't you?'

Lingo murmured something in the affirmative and continued to kiss her into a state of speechlessness. But he had a sudden horrid vision of Phil, making one of her scenes, in the flat this morning before he had come to Delia.

They had been singularly impolite to each other and when Lingo had murmured the word 'separation', Phil had snapped:

'Don't be a damned fool. We're up to our eyes in debt and we can't afford to separate. If I can find a rich man you can be quite sure I'll be the first to quit. And if you can find a rich woman — the same thing applies. But it's no good you wasting your time with the Beringham girl. She hasn't a bean.'

Before he left Delia, however, he felt that he had been wonderful to her. She was much less nervy and unhappy. So touching, the way she relied on him.

Delia, as she kissed him good-bye, thought:

'I needn't feel lost and helpless — with Lingo. He'll always make me happy — he always does.'

Delia was much more self-possessed than Martin had seen her since her father's death when he came to lunch with her after the funeral. Some of the bewilderment and shock had left her. Her nerves were not so badly on edge.

Martin was still suffering from the effects of the funeral but he tried not to depress Delia. She, however, insisted upon discussing her father's affairs, and over their coffee and cigarettes they talked of the future.

'It's certain now that I shall have nothing but my own personal possessions once this house is sold up,' said Delia. 'Isn't it?'

'I'm afraid so, my dear,' he said.

'Then the sooner I get out of here, the better.'

'Frankly, yes. You mustn't run into any more debt.'

'The shops will see to that,' said Delia with a twisted smile, and told him the story about Pacquille.

His grey, serious eyes rested on her with compassion.

'So you've come up against it already — poor dear.'

'Well — it doesn't much matter. It *would* have hurt me so much more if I hadn't had Lingo.'

Martin Revell looked away from the lovely young figure. He did not want to look at her, to watch her face soften at the mention of that man's name.

'Have you and Hewes come to any definite decision yet, Delia?' Martin asked with an effort.

Delia helped herself to more sugar and stirred the crystals into the hot black coffee thoughtfully. She answered him:

'In a way — yes. He sat with me this morning, you know, and we talked while — ' She broke off, her under-lip quivering.

Martin looked at her with tenderness.

'Yes, my dear, don't think of it — '

'Well — we talked things over and of course it's quite decided that Lingo is going to get a divorce and marry me.

The only thing is — we're not quite certain what to do meanwhile.'

Martin did not look at her. He took a packet of cigarettes from his pocket and lit one. Then he said:

'Must *you* be brought into the divorce?'

'I expect so — if I go away with Lingo. Naturally his wife will cite me, won't she? But who cares?'

Martin stared at the floor blindly.

Delia looked at him.

'Martin — you needn't look like that — I'm going to be quite all right — I assure you.'

'All right — you must do as you please,' he said curtly. 'I can only beg you to be careful.'

Delia flushed.

'I'll let you know what Lingo and I decide,' she said coldly.

'Please do.'

'Meanwhile you must get on with the disposal of all Daddy's possessions, I presume.'

'The official receiver will see to that.'

'It all sounds beastly. I don't understand it, but I suppose the sooner I move out of here the better. I expect I can put up with the Willises. Betty's been a dear. She's lunching with her people today and I think she's going to suggest my staying there for a bit.'

Martin turned to face her now, grimly.

'Betty is a broad-minded young woman, but Colonel Willis belongs to the old school. I've met him. Forgive me if I'm brutal, my child, but if he knows about you and Hewes — '

'Don't go on,' she broke in, 'I know what you mean. If Colonel Willis doesn't approve he needn't have me there. I don't care.'

She was so proud, so sure of herself. Martin, who had battled with life and seen behind the scenes, looked at her half in anger, half in pity, wholly in love.

'I'm going to spend this afternoon sorting out some of my personal possessions,' Delia announced. 'I can keep my own things, can't I?'

'Yes.'

'I can sell my jewels if necessary. And my sable jacket — and my Alfa Romeo.'

'Yes,' he repeated. 'Anything that legally belongs to you.'

Delia bit her lower lip. But she kept her head high.

'It will be — jolly, won't it?'

He wanted to sympathise and was at a loss for something to say. She forestalled him by her next words.

'It would have been hellish — without Lingo.'

Martin looked grimly at his wristwatch.

'I must fly, Delia. There's work at the office.'

'Thanks awfully for — this morning — ' she said and added awkwardly: 'Thanks for everything you've done.'

'Will you remember that if you've nowhere else to go I'd like awfully for you to come along to us for a bit. Aunt Eva and Elinor would love to have you.'

'It's very kind of them,' said Delia. 'And by the way, please thank your aunt for the awfully nice letter she sent me when Daddy died. I'm going to answer it — but I've felt so dazed — I haven't written to anybody yet.'

'She'll understand that,' said Martin gently.

Delia's long and lovely lashes drooped a little. For a moment she conjured up a vision of Martin's home. His mother had died while he was still a small boy at his preparatory school.

And then Mrs. Warnleigh, Aunt Eva, who was herself a widow, had come to the Revells' house in Hampstead to look after her brother and the small boy. Now that Martin's father was dead he continued to live there in Hampstead with his aunt.

Delia liked Mrs. Warnleigh. She was a very charming and a very interesting woman, nearing the sixties. But she did not altogether understand the new, easy conventions and principles of young people of the twentieth century. In consequence Delia did not feel that she could ever behave quite naturally with her. On the other hand Aunt Eva, whatever her own standards, was never bitter or censorious about others whose opinions differed from her. She had always been charming to Delia and Delia would not have minded staying with her.

But there was also Elinor in the household — and Elinor definitely bored Delia. She was Aunt Eva's adopted daughter, about the same age as Martin and — in Delia's opinion — an incredibly dull young woman. Worthy, of course. Did lots of good works and was always sacrificing something for someone. Delia was quite sure that Elinor was deeply in love with Martin and sometimes she wondered why Martin did not marry her. She had no 'chic', no idea what clothes to buy or how to put them on. But she had quite a good figure, good teeth and skin, and masses of fair hair which she refused to shingle. She wore it in a bun which made her look much older than she was.

Delia imagined that Martin would have been impressed by Elinor's worthiness. But he never seemed to display any more than a brotherly feeling for her. Queer creatures, men, Delia decided.

'Don't forget there's a bed for you at Hampstead when you want one,' were Martin's parting words.

'Heaps of thanks,' Delia answered, with real gratitude softening her eyes. 'But I expect I'll go to Betty — or possibly straight to Lingo.'

Martin Revell left the Beringhams' luxurious house a very harassed and troubled young man. And he walked down Charles Street with a black, almost murderous hatred in his heart for Lingo Hewes.

Delia sat in the middle of the floor of her big bedroom. A strange position for Delia, but the best one under the circumstances. The room was in chaos. There was no carpet to be seen.

Delia was leaving the lovely house in

Charles Street this afternoon and going to stay with Betty.

Now she was trying to sort her things and pack. She had never had to do such a thing in her life before, waited upon hand and foot since her babyhood.

Her face was flushed and puckered. She felt shamefully helpless.

'God knows what I'm going to do with all these odds and ends — I'm sure I haven't enough trunks to hold them,' she groaned.

From Betty Willis, who was at the other side of the room, kneeling beside a suitcase, came a sympathetic groan.

'It's *too* frightful, darling. You'll have to put a bundle of the things you don't like in a sheet and pack 'em off to a secondhand clothes dealer, so far as I can see.'

Delia drew a hand across her forehead wearily.

'Marie always used to dispose of my things when I got tired of them. Where does one go to sell cast-offs?'

'You'd better bring them home

— we'll ask Doris.'

'You're lucky to have Doris,' said Delia. 'I never realised before what a rock poor Marie was to lean on.'

'I'm afraid *I'm* not much good to lean on,' said Betty. 'I'm about as stupid as you are at these sort of times, my sweet.'

'We've both been spoiled, that's what it is,' said Delia in a low voice.

Betty got up, picked her way daintily through a confusion of things and sat down on the floor beside her friend.

'Darling, cheer up,' Betty said, putting an arm around her. 'It's going to be all right — it's beastly for you now — but you've tons of friends left — it isn't as though you're alone in the world.'

Delia pressed her lips together. She blinked back the tears.

She looked at Betty with hard, bright eyes.

'I'm all right. Don't worry. And you needn't call yourself stupid — you've been marvellous to me, Betty. But I'm afraid Martin was right. I haven't got so many friends as I thought I had. I've called twice at Diana Warrington's — she and her husband were always here when Daddy was alive. And she's been '*out*' both times. And I happen to know that both times she was *in*. She's obviously one of the ones who don't want to know me any more because of what poor Daddy did.'

'She isn't worth worrying about.'

'No,' said Delia with a hard little laugh. 'And there's Connie Berrell — she used to chase me morning and night in the old days. Last night, while you were out, Lingo and I dropped in at Connie's flat at the usual cocktail time. Two people that I know pretended not to see me when I entered the drawing-room and Connie was quite different — called me 'darling' and admired my frock — oh, yes! But she was *different* — ' Delia gulped and clenched her hands. 'I tell you I'm beginning to know who my friends are.'

'Well, you know I am,' said Betty.

'And Martin is, and Lingo.'

Delia, whose slim body had been taut, relaxed, and smiled — rather a strained smile.

'I certainly know you are. And of course Martin. But Lingo — is much more.'

'What have you and Lingo decided to do?'

'He's coming to see me at tea-time — he's going to tell me then how long the divorce will take and we're going to make arrangements for the future. Thank God for Lingo — what would I have done without him!'

Betty Willis rose and stepped carefully through the chaos in the beautiful bedroom, found a cigarette from an ivory box on the dressing-table and lit it.

'Well, my lamb,' she said with a sigh, and turned back to the disconsolate young figure in the black cocktail suit, 'I suppose we'd better get on with the good work. It's eleven o'clock and we want to get this job finished so that we can leave the house after tea.'

Delia mentally shook herself, rose and stretched her arms above her head.

'Come on then! Who cares! It's a new experience for little me to be up and doing at this hour of the morning, anyhow.'

'Shame!' said Betty in her slightly drawling voice.

Somebody knocked at the door.

'Come in!' said Delia.

Florrie, the 'tweeny, with a smudge on her cheek and many holes in her apron, stood with a note in her hand.

'A note for Miss Willis,' she said.

'What on earth about?' said Betty, then when she looked at the envelope: 'Gracious! It's from my female parent.'

Delia knelt in front of a wardrobe trunk and began to fold, very badly, a nylon blouse which would just fit in one of the drawers.

'Well I'm damned!' Betty's voice, indignant and without its accustomed drawl, made Delia turn round and look up at her.

'My dear — what on earth — '

Betty's sleepy eyes opened more widely than usual and she looked pink and angry. She folded up the letter which she had been reading and thrust it into the pocket of her exquisitely tailored suit.

'I shall never forgive Father for this.'

Delia stared.

'But what's he done? What's it all about?'

'It's iniquitous!' exclaimed Betty.

'For goodness' sake tell me.'

'I can hardly face you.'

Delia looked at her uneasily.

'Is it to do with me?'

'Yes — darling I'm so ashamed of Father.'

'My dear old thing — don't be afraid — tell me. You know nothing can spoil our friendship.'

Betty stammered an explanation. Her mother had sent this letter round to her in a panic. Colonel Willis had, apparently, come down to breakfast, opened his mail and exploded after reading a letter from his sister. The sister, Betty's Aunt Agatha, who was a 'Bridge-fiend', had recently been playing contract at a party which included Mrs. Lionel Hewes. At this juncture the vivid pink colour rushed to Delia's face. She interrupted by saying, softly:

'Lingo's wife — my lord!'

Betty stammered on. Aunt Agatha said in her letter that Phyllis Hewes was a delightful woman and one of her best friends. She was very unhappy because that bounder of a husband of hers was behaving in a disgraceful manner with a slip of a girl named Delia Beringham. Aunt Agatha knew that Delia had been at school with Betty and advised her brother not to countenance any friendship between the two girls in the future. It wouldn't be nice for Betty to be seen about with a girl whose name was linked with that of a married man.

'Wouldn't it be nice!' repeated Betty, blazing. 'My God — the old brute! How dare she try and order my life about. She's the head of our family and the most interfering hag. Father listens to everything she says and now Mother says in her letter that he forbade her to have you to stay with us. Delia — darling — I'm simply livid — '

Delia stood up.

'That's all right, Betty darling. I know perfectly well that it's nothing to do with you. It's just — bad luck — that Mrs. Hewes should be a friend of your aunt's. It only shows one how news travels. And it defeats me — absolutely defeats me — because Lingo swore his wife *wanted* a divorce.'

'You can't believe a word anybody says!'

'Apparently not. But I thought I could believe what Lingo said. I shall have to ask him about it.'

'I don't know that you can believe what Aunt Agatha says. Anyhow things get exaggerated when they're repeated. And I daresay Mrs. Lingo likes to parade as the injured wife even if she does want a divorce.'

'Perhaps,' said Delia in a low voice.

But her heart was jerking in a horrid, worried way. She felt curiously frightened, all of a sudden.

At a quarter to four Lingo Hewes called for the last time at the house in Charles Street — a house which, he admitted as he approached it, had once been the mecca of his ambitions and was now the grave of them.

Upstairs at her bedroom window, Delia saw Lingo arrive.

She ran downstairs to welcome him, feeling that it would have been the end of the world for her had he not come.

When she stepped into the morning-room where Lingo waited for her she looked, as he told himself, like 'a million dollars' rather than a girl without a shilling in the world.

She was enchanting in the silver-grey jersey dress, with touches of cherry red at throat and wrists and a little cherry-coloured beret on the side of the smooth black head. Over her arm she carried a grey coat which belonged to the dress; a lovely thing with a beautiful long collar of mink.

'What a damn shame the old man did in all the cash,' Lingo thought gloomily. But he greeted Delia with more than usual warmth.

'My sweet! My poor sweet!'

She choked back the tears which had been close to the surface all day long. Dropping the coat on a chair, she rushed into Lingo's arms.

'Don't cry, angel!' he murmured.

She lifted her head and showed eyes that sparkled with unshed tears.

'I'm not going to. But, oh, Lingo, I've wanted you frightfully today. It's marvellous to see you. I've had such a depressing morning. Betty and I have been sorting out all my things and packing — and it all sort of rushed over me suddenly that everything's gone — the whole of my old life — it terrifies me.'

'My poor darling.'

She looked up at him and gave a little sigh as she drew comfort from the ardour in his eyes and the soothing touch of the hand which was caressing her.

'But it's all different now you're here. Lingo, what *would* I have done without you?'

'My sweet!'

She stared mournfully round the room.

'Let's sit down and talk,' she said, and pulled a dust-sheet off one of the chairs and led him to it. She perched herself on the arm, keeping a hand locked in his.

'We've got so much to talk about and decide,' she added.

He raised an eyebrow and felt for his cigarette-case.

'Smoke?' he asked her.

'No. Not just now.'

'Would you like to come out to tea? The house rather gives me the creeps this afternoon.'

She felt that, too, but she tried to laugh.

'Yes, I know. But I don't want to go out. At least, not just yet. We're alone here and I must talk to you. You see — I've got to decide what to do and I can't do anything until I hear what *you* want me to do. I'm absolutely in your hands now, Lingo darling.'

He lit a cigarette.

'You're going to the Willises for a bit, aren't you?' he said uneasily.

She bit hard at her lip. Her small fingers tightened over his hand.

'That *was* the arrangement. But I'm afraid it's cancelled.'

Lingo did not look at her.

'Oh? Why?'

She explained. The colour stung her cheeks and her heart beat faster as she recounted the story of Betty's Aunt Agatha and the scandal at the Bridge party.

'You see, darling,' she finished with a wry smile, 'Colonel Willis is a Victorian and he doesn't approve of a girl who is going to be cited in a divorce case.'

It was Lingo's turn to flush. Scarlet to the roots of his fair hair he continued to stare at the carpet and smoke.

'That infernal woman, Connie Berrell, again,' he said between his teeth.

'Perhaps. But I don't quite understand why your wife complained to Betty's aunt. I thought she was only too anxious to have a divorce, Lingo.'

Lingo cleared his throat.

'Yes — yes, so she is. My dear girl, one can't take any notice of the things that are said at a woman's Bridge party. Half of 'em only play for the sake of the gossip in between the rubbers.'

'But you see Betty's aunt *did* take notice, and this is the result. I'm taboo in the Willis household.'

'Damn shame,' muttered Lingo.

She put an arm around his shoulders, bent down and laid a cheek against his hair.

'Don't think I mind — really — so long as I've got you, Lingo. After all, I knew what I was in for when I first agreed to run away with you. But that bit about your wife being unhappy — that upset me.'

Lingo made no answer for a moment.

It struck Delia that he was curiously silent and unresponsive to her caresses.

'What's the matter, Lingo?'

'Nothing.'

'Look at me, darling.'

He lifted his head reluctantly. But his gaze only met hers for a fraction of an instant then wavered again.

'This is all infernally awkward,' he stammered.

'Awkward?' she repeated. 'You mean about — what your wife is saying?'

'I mean the whole show.'

Her heart seemed to miss a beat.

'Lingo, what do you mean?'

He moved restlessly away from her encircling arm.

'Don't you see, my sweet, how awkward it is!'

'Lingo, isn't it true that your wife wants a divorce?'

'Certainly she wants it. We don't begin to get on. But it's this ghastly question of cash.'

Delia's cheeks were now burning pink, and she sat up very straight and still on the arm of the chair.

'If I had money — the whole damn thing would be so simple,' Lingo added. 'We could just snap our fingers at the lot of them and move off. But as it is — ' He shrugged his shoulders and left the sentence unfinished.

'One moment,' said Delia. She slipped from the arm of the chair and stood in front of him, one hand held nervously to her throat. 'You're frightening me, Lingo. All this talk about money — I don't understand — we've never talked about money before. The question hasn't arisen between us.'

'My dear child — naturally not — I mean to say — ' He stuttered and broke off.

Her eyes dilated.

'Lingo — you don't mean that because Daddy — because *I* haven't any money now — *Lingo*! You're not trying to tell me that makes any difference to *you*.'

He dared not look at her.

'It's devilish difficult to explain, darling. I know we've never talked about money in the past. But we've got to face facts a bit today. I'm hard up. I must be honest with you. Phil and I are both on the extravagant side and we live beyond our income. I just can't afford a divorce — that's all.'

She stared down at him, her heart beating so fast that it made her breathing difficult.

He stubbed his cigarette end in an ash-tray and stood up.

He caught her hand and pulled her towards him.

'My sweet — angel — come here — let me hold you. Darling — this is the very deuce. I'm damned sorry. Nobody's sorrier than I am. But you see, I simply could not afford to let Phil divorce me, pay the costs, give her a third of my income and support you as well. It's absolutely out of the question. Try and understand.'

She stood rigid in the circle of his arms.

'You mean that — you were relying on *my* money.'

'Oh — that's rather crude, my sweet — '

'Hadn't we better be crude,' she interrupted, breathing very fast. 'I think it will be better to dispense with the frills now. I've been content with the frills too long. It's time I had sense enough to look underneath. The truth is this: When you suggested running away with me you thought my father would help us. Now you know that he can't — you don't want to go away with me. Answer me, Lingo. Isn't that the truth?'

'Look here — '

'No!' she broke in violently. 'Don't haver. Answer my question, Lingo, once and for all.'

He released her and shrugged his shoulders.

'Very well — if you must be so blunt,' he said haughtily.

She nodded slowly.

'I see,' she said. 'Well now I know.

I'm glad I do. I should have hated to have been married — for my money!' She gave a choked little laugh and added: 'But I needn't be afraid of that now, need I?'

Lingo began to feel quite offended by her attitude. He had no idea how to deal with this strange Delia who was all white and angry and shaking, talking to him in an icy, intolerant fashion.

'Martin was right,' said Delia. 'And he's been right nearly all the way along.'

'Don't throw Revell's name down my throat, *please*,' Lingo protested.

'And I was so sure that *you* — ' her voice broke — '*you* of all people — '

He forgot to be haughty. Her face was all screwed up like a child's and he was stirred, again, to all the real feeling of which he was capable. He caught her back in his arms and held her close.

'Angel — don't look like that. You can rely on me. I'm terribly in love with you. The question of money doesn't alter that fact at all. Look here, my sweet, it doesn't matter a jot about the

Willises or anybody else. You're all packed up, aren't you? Well it won't take me long to pack. We'll cross over to Paris, tonight. I'm not so broke that I can't afford to raise enough for that. And of course when my uncle, old Chiselmay, pegs out — I shall be coming into the money *and* the title. Everything will be all right then. Kiss me, my sweet — we can't quarrel, you and I. Can we?'

For a moment she leaned against him.

'You mean — you still want to go through with the divorce for me?'

He laughed self-consciously.

'My dear, why worry about the divorce? Why worry about anything but the present? And the fact that we are madly in love with each other?'

The last shred of confidence, of faith, died abruptly within her.

She drew away from him. She said:

'You mean, you'd just like me to — have a week or two with you in Paris.'

'Oh, longer than that, if the money will hold out.'

A long, tense silence. Then Delia, white to the lips, whispered three words:

'*You* — miserable *creature*!'

Scarlet, embarrassed, he tried to capitulate.

'Darling — really — you're not going to pretend you're as prim as Betty's aunt — or friend Revell! Damn it all — I thought you were broad-minded — and I thought you cared for me.'

She trembled from head to foot.

'Get out of this house, Lingo. Go on — get out! And don't dare talk to me about Martin. Because if he were here — he'd *kick* you out.'

Lingo gave her one look, then picked up his hat and a paper he had just bought.

'Oh, very well. If that's how you feel about things. But you're behaving rather stupidly and I think you'll be sorry for it when I've gone.'

She did not answer.

At half-past five Delia walked into the offices of Revell & Revell, solicitors, for the first time in her life.

She had come to Martin's office out of sheer necessity. He was, after all, her father's executor and a family friend. He alone knew what possessions she had which were of value, and which she meant to sell, and he could advance her a small sum of money. It took time to sell things and she was in urgent need of ready cash.

She went into Martin's office. The door was closed behind her. Martin had risen from his chair and was facing her. It struck her even in the midst of her tragedy, how important he looked, dear old Martin, in this imposing room with its red Turkey carpet, and the big mahogany desk which was covered with papers — legal documents neatly tied and lettered — and a large bookcase full of heavy volumes. On the grey walls hung a set of rather nice coloured prints depicting famous Judges in the Old Bailey.

Martin held out his hand.

'Delia, my dear, what an unexpected pleasure!'

Mechanically she gave him her hand in return. He pressed it warmly. His heart was beating fast at the sight of her. But that was not for her to know. He said:

'It's the first time you've ever been here. Come and sit down. Here in my big chair. It's quite comfortable.'

She smiled a little but refused the chair and sat on the edge of the desk. There was going to be a fight between Martin and herself in a moment and she knew it. So she girt herself with what weapons she possessed.

'You look very imposing here, Martin,' were her first words to him.

He laughed.

'I feel anything but imposing. I'm like a fish out of water. My father and circumstances made a lawyer of me, Delia, but I'd rather have been something quite the antithesis.'

'What's the exact opposite of a

lawyer?' She spoke lightly. 'Let's think — the law always seems to me dull and dry and unromantic. Therefore you wish you'd been a musician or a poet!'

He laughed again, a trifle self-consciously, and thrust his hands in his pockets.

'I certainly love music — and poetry.'

'You aren't by any chance a money-lender?'

'No — why?' He laughed again. 'Money-lending isn't romantic, is it?'

'Far from it. But often a necessity, I imagine.'

The feeling of exhilaration which he had had when she first came into the room, bringing with her that beauty and freshness and faint perfume which glorified his sombre room, died down. He no longer smiled. He said gravely:

'Have you come to see me about anything special, Delia?'

She swung crossed, slender legs and shrugged her shoulders, nervous and troubled, despite all her efforts to appear otherwise.

'Yes. I've come to turn you into a money-lender.'

'My dear.' At once he was concerned for her and businesslike. 'But of course — you have only to ask — '

She did not look at him. A very real colour burnt through the rouge on her cheeks.

'Only a loan, Martin. You see I haven't been able to sell any of my things yet. I scarcely know where I stand and these things take time. I'm terribly short of cash — ' She laughed and bit her under-lip. 'Just a few pounds to rub along with.'

'My dear!' he said again, his thin, clever face was red now, like hers, and his heart torn with pity for her. Perhaps she read the pity in his eyes, because immediately she warded it off by joking.

'You must consider yourself my uncle or my guardian for the moment. Little Delia needs some pocket-money.'

She was laughing. Rather callous about the situation, he thought, and was absurdly annoyed because she used the word 'uncle'. He was not so very much older than she was and he was in love with her — desperately — hopelessly in love.

'How much do you want?' he asked. 'Anything — just tell me, Delia.'

'What do you think I should get for my sports car — seven-year-old Alfa Romeo in perfect condition? Smithson — ' Delia's voice quivered slightly as she mentioned the name of her father's chauffeur. It conjured up such visions of the past, dead past. 'Smithson kept it beautifully.'

'I know, my dear,' said Martin with quick sympathy, 'but second-hand cars sell for nothing. It's iniquitous, but I'm afraid your Alfa won't fetch more than a third of its value.'

'Well, I've got some diamonds — all the rings and so-on that belonged to Mummy — ' she bit fiercely at her lip although she kept her head held high. 'It's horrible to have to part with them but I suppose I've got to.'

'Delia, my dear — '

Impulsively he was moving towards her.

But she would not have his sympathy.

'It's all in the day's work,' she interrupted him. 'I don't really mind. Just tell me where to find an honest buyer.'

'Let me have the jewels you want to sell and I'll do what I can for you. And I'll deal with the car, too, if you'd like me to.'

'Thanks, Martin, it's decent of you.'

He frowned and looked away from her.

'Now that I know I can bank on a hundred or two, I shan't mind so much asking you for a loan,' she said.

'Why shouldn't you mind asking me, anyhow,' he exclaimed. 'Surely we're old enough friends for that, Delia.'

She took a small gold case from her bag, found a cigarette and put it between her lips, then gave an almost flippant smile.

'I've often heard that the best way to lose your friends is to borrow from them.'

He lit the cigarette for her and saw that the small hand, with its tapered fingers and polished nails, was shaking.

He answered, a trifle grimly.

'I think you've got it a bit wrong. You lose your friends more easily when you lend money to them.'

'Aren't we cynical. Never mind, Martin. *I* won't be ungrateful.'

'I never for a moment suggested that you would be. I wasn't being personal.'

'Dear old Martin, don't get cross.'

He felt himself growing hot. Gloomily he sat down at the desk. He opened a drawer and unlocked a dispatch case.

'I can let you have twenty-five pounds cash and I'll send you some more tomorrow,' he said.

'Marvellous. I'm richer than I expected.'

He counted out the notes and gave them to her.

Delia put the notes in her bag.

'It really is nice of you to do this, Martin.'

He looked up at her.

'Delia,' he said suddenly. 'You said something just now about getting a job. Does that mean your plans have altered?'

Now for trouble, she thought, and faced the difficult moment which she had anticipated when she entered Martin's office.

'Yes.'

'You told me you were going to stay with Betty Willis. Are you?'

'Not now. They can't have me.'

'Or won't,' ran through his brain, remembering his own warning to her about Colonel Willis's Victorian outlook. Aloud he said: 'I see. Then where are you going?'

'I'm at the Grosvenor at the moment.'

'Why there?'

'Oh, just for the night. I shall find something cheaper tomorrow.'

'And when do you intend to — let Hewes look after you?' He put the question, hating every word of it, and hating all that it implied.

Then Delia's thick lashes hid what lay in her eyes.

'I don't know that he *is* going to look after me.'

Martin caught his breath.

'Oh? Have you changed your mind about him?'

It would have been more than she could have endured to answer truthfully and tell him that it was Lingo who had changed *his* mind about her. But it would be too humiliating to let Martin know that Lingo's love had not been able to stand the test of poverty.

'I don't know that I've exactly changed,' she said, shrugging her shoulders. 'But things are a bit different because — well — Lingo doesn't think his wife is willing to divorce him and so — well — we can scarcely marry, can we?'

She was stumbling a little over the words. Martin, never taking his gaze from her, clenched a hand behind his back. He felt that he knew all that she would not tell him. He heard her say lightly:

'I don't suppose Lingo and I will see much of each other in the future.'

'I only hope that's true,' Martin said under his breath.

Delia gave a short laugh.

'Aren't you solemn about it!'

'You were going to take a solemn step, and quite frankly I hated the idea of you marrying Hewes.'

'Oh, marriage!' said Delia scornfully as though the word meant nothing to her. 'What's in it? People who marry never seem to get on very well. I think I was rather foolish to even think of marrying Lingo. A gay week in Paris might have been more to the point.'

She spoke a little wildly, insolently, anything to mask her misery and the pride which Lingo had wounded so horribly. But Martin without understanding, looked at her aghast.

'Delia!'

'Aren't you easily shocked!'

'No,' he said angrily, 'but I hate to hear you talking like a little fool, especially when I know you don't mean it.'

She slipped from the desk and stubbed the end of a half-smoked cigarette in an ash-tray. Her cheeks were still burning.

'Well, as long as you know I don't mean it, you needn't worry.'

'But I am worried about you.'

There was a real note of anxiety in the roughness of his voice which suddenly touched her.

'You needn't be. You're sweet to me, Martin, and I've been a little pig.'

'If only you would marry me — '

But scarcely were the words out of his mouth than he regretted them. A look more bitter than he cared to see came over that young, charming face.

'My *dear* — of course I won't marry you. How sweet and quixotic of you! But really, 'The Orphan of the Storm' will manage to look after herself quite well.'

Martin got his feelings under rein again. But he felt maddened. She added:

'I don't think I shall ever marry. I'm afraid I haven't much faith left in men.'

She walked to the window and looked out at the sunshine blindly. Her head was aching — her heart too.

She turned round and faced him.

'Well, I'd better run along. You've got a client, I know.'

'You're so independent,' he said with a sharp sigh. 'Where will it lead you?'

'I shall rub along.'

'But you've never been alone — never had to face things like this — '

'Then it's time I learned. Haven't you told me hundreds of times that I used to waste my time and frivol my life away? Now I'm hoping to take a job.'

'What sort?' he asked, torn with anxiety for her.

'I'll let you know what I get. And I'm going to prove to you that I'm not as useless or so frivolous as you thought I was.'

He saw that it was hopeless to argue with her.

'I don't mind what you do so long as you take care of yourself.'

'You're really a dear,' she said, more moved that she cared to show.

And that ended their interview.

2

Two weeks later.

A wet, windy day and not at all the sort of weather one expected in August. It was even cold, and Delia was shivering when she stepped off the bus at the corner of Mapledon Road which ran into Dorset Square. During this last fortnight she had tried to accustom herself to buses but she still chafed impotently when she had to stand at the corner of a street in the pouring rain and wait with a crowd for a bus to come along; then, when she got into it, find herself jammed amongst a mass of wet, unfriendly humanity.

Everything had changed! She had found a cheap hotel here, the 'Moderna' in Mapledon Road, which seemed to her a horrible place although it was quiet and ultra-respectable. With all her heart she hated it. But it was cheap and she had not the heart to set out and find anything else. She was too busy trying to find work.

This afternoon as she walked from the bus to the hotel she faced the realisation that work was the most difficult thing in the world to find — difficult even when one was skilled in some trade. Almost impossible when one knew nothing.

Up in her hateful bedroom with its worn linoleum and ugly furniture, Delia sat down on the edge of her bed to read her afternoon post.

There were two letters. One from Betty from Scotland. The Willis family had gone up to Ayrshire to the Colonel's grousemoor. Betty wrote in her usual devoted strain, full of anxiety for her friend, which could not fail to touch Delia. At times like these one certainly learned who were one's true friends and who were not.

Tears were stinging her eyelids when she finished Betty's long epistle from Scotland. Then she took up the second letter which had come. It bore a French stamp. She opened it eagerly. This was from 'Melly' — in other words Mademoiselle Duplais who had been her governess when she was a little girl of thirteen. A nice creature whom she had affectionately nicknamed 'Melly' and never forgotten after she left the family and went back to her home in Dieppe.

A few days ago, in despair about her future, Delia had written to Melly and told her what had happened. Here was the reply.

Melly wrote just as Delia would have expected. She expressed herself profoundly shocked and grieved by the dire news from her *chère petite* Delia. She suggested at once that Delia should go over to Dieppe and stay with her in the little house which she shared with her married sister.

Her health was in a bad state, she said, and of late she had not been taking any work but she felt certain that Delia would find a position in Dieppe. As governess, maybe, to some little

French child. Melly would do her utmost or at any rate would adore to see her treasured charge of former years.

When Delia folded up the thin sheet of letter with its slanting, delicate handwriting which recalled happier days of her childhood, her tears were falling fast.

She brushed them away, half ashamed of her sentimentality. Her tears were always so close to the surface now, and she was easily touched by little kindnesses. That was not like the old Delia.

'You must get a grip on yourself, my child,' she reflected. 'You're becoming sloppy!'

But Melly's letter had given her an idea. It would be better — nicer in every way — to find work abroad if she could. Melly was a darling and in that modest home in Dieppe she knew she would find a warm welcome awaiting her.

'I shall go to Dieppe — at once,'

Delia told herself. 'Away from everybody who has ever known me in Town.'

Once she conceived the idea that she wanted to go to Dieppe, she acted without further delay. There was nothing to keep her here in this hateful hotel or in London which was, nowadays, hateful too, nobody whom she particularly minded leaving. After tea she rushed out to the nearest shipping agency to inquire about boats.

She had her passport ready. A passport which awoke many recollections. She had travelled all over the Continent with that dear, dead father who had been such a brilliant failure. She had enough money for the moment. She was told at the touring-agency that she could catch the night-boat from Newhaven to Dieppe if she wanted to. She would have to be on board by ten and she could either disembark in the early hours of the morning or sleep on board until eight o'clock. It was the cheapest way.

'Then I shall go,' said Delia.

The clerk at the bureau, who had been talking to one of his colleagues, returned to her.

'I understand that there's a very bad gale blowing in the Channel at the moment,' he said. 'There's just a chance that the service will be suspended.'

But Delia was not to be swerved from her purpose now. Storm or no storm she would catch the boat-train and if she found that the service was suspended, she would come back or put up in Newhaven for the night, and sail the next morning.

She purchased her ticket, booked a berth in the ladies' cabin and rushed back to the Moderna Hotel to pack, less depressed than she had felt for some time.

'I'll write to Martin from Dieppe tomorrow,' she told herself. 'And I'll let him know how things stand and what chances I've got of a job out there, once I've seen Melly.'

She paid her bill at the hotel with a feeling of utter thankfulness that she was leaving it now that the time had come.

It was not until she reached Newhaven that she discovered that an unkind fate had brought her in contact with the one person in the world from whom she most wanted to fly.

When she was one of the crowd jostling through the Customs, standing in a queue waiting to have her passport stamped, she caught sight of a tall, fair-haired man just in front of her. A figure all too familiar; spruce as ever in his beautiful grey suit and travelling coat and well-polished tan shoes; soft hat set a little insolently on the side of his handsome head.

Lingo! *Lingo!* Carrying a suitcase and very obviously bent on the same object as herself. He, too, was crossing to Dieppe.

For a moment Delia's heart seemed to stand still and the blood sang in her temples. Why, why should this have happened? The very person whom she most wanted to avoid here, just about to step on the boat with her! And a boat was such a small place; it would be so difficult not to be seen by him.

But Lingo saw her long before she got through the Custom-house. When his passport had been stamped he stepped aside to light a cigarette and his roving eye caught sight of the slim, attractive girl passing through the barrier. The cigarette was never lighted. He gave an exclamation and started forward.

'Delia!' he said under his breath.

Delia saw that it was futile to even attempt to avoid or ignore Lingo. His blue eyes were looking at her hard and he acknowledged her with an eager smile as though they had never agreed to part.

Then he was at her side, doffing his hat in the graceful manner which she had once thought so attractive.

'My dear old thing — what a surprise! You could knock me down with a feather. Where are you going? Paris?'

'No, Dieppe,' she said in the steadiest voice she could muster.

'But, my dear, what tremendous luck running into you like this,' said Lingo's drawling voice. 'What luggage have you? Can I help?'

'Thanks, no. The porter has my trunk.'

'But where are you off to?' he persisted, undaunted by her coldness.

'To Dieppe, I told you.'

'All alone?'

'I don't see that it concerns you,' she said in a freezing voice.

He flushed, then laughed and shrugged his shoulders.

'Aren't we going to be friends for old time's sake?'

She gave him a quick, indignant look.

'You seem to have no sense of shame.'

'Why should I be ashamed?'

'No, perhaps you wouldn't see any necessity. You can have no sense of shame. Otherwise you wouldn't have behaved so badly.'

'My dear girl,' he drawled. 'Dash it all — if a fellow hasn't a cent, he can't very well come up to scratch, can he? As I told you — a divorce costs money.'

'I refuse to reopen this discussion,' she interrupted, and felt herself trembling. 'I told you what I thought of you when we last met. Leave it at that.'

'My dear,' he said softly. 'Don't be stupid. There's no need for melodramatics. We're both crossing over to Dieppe tonight — let's be friendly about it even if we don't agree.'

Delia mastered herself.

'If it amuses you to talk to me now — go ahead. As soon as I am on board I'm going down into the ladies' cabin to sleep. I'm afraid they won't allow you in there.'

'What bad luck, as there's so much youth and beauty about. Phew! There's a gale blowing. I should think the damn boat will sink. And that'll be the end of us, my sweet!'

The endearment made Delia grit her teeth.

'People who haven't a cent aren't much use in the world, my dear Lingo, so if either you or I sink, I doubt if we shall be missed.'

He gave her an amused look.

'You've become quite a cynic, my dear.'

She ignored that and paid attention to the porter who was carrying her trunk up the gangway.

Lingo seemed determined to pursue her and kept close to her as they stepped on to the boat.

'You're a good sailor, aren't you, Delia? Don't know that I am very. Don't like the idea of this wind. It's going to be damned rough.'

'I hope so,' she said with a queer, hard laugh.

'The only consolation is,' said Lingo, 'that I'm off for a week alone. I'm sick of Phil's tantrums. I need a little jollity. Can't afford it, but it's cheaper coming this way than flying. Look here, Delia, I don't know where you're off to, but why don't you come along with me — '

She turned on him furiously, then controlled herself and laughed.

'What a persistent nature you've got, Lingo.'

'I'm still in love with you.'

She gave him a withering look.

'You amuse me. However, forgive me if I go and settle myself in my berth. Good-bye.'

'Then you won't be friendly?'

She looked him straight in the eyes, then:

'If you want to know the truth, Lingo, I find it quite impossible to be friendly with you. I think you're the most despicable man I've ever met in my life.'

A moment's silence. Then Lingo gave a queer little laugh.

'Straight from the shoulder. I don't think you're as sweet as you used to be, Delia. Don't let yourself become sour, my dear, because it doesn't suit you.'

She gasped a little. The man's

insolence was colossal. Without saying another word she turned and walked along the deck towards the ladies' saloon.

Lingo stayed on deck a moment, watching the crane swing the baggage off the dock into the hold. His thoughts about Delia were not singularly pleasant.

Suddenly his gaze lit on the figure of a man in a dark overcoat, hurrying up the gangway, and his eyes widened with astonishment.

Here was another coincidence. That man was surely Martin Revell. Did Delia know he was coming on board? He presumed that she did. Perhaps that was why she had snubbed him so unmercifully.

Lingo faded away into the shadows where Martin could not see him and betook himself to the saloon where he could get a strong drink. He was quite certain that already he was feeling a little sick.

Earlier that same afternoon Martin

Revell had journeyed from London to Brighton to see an old and valued client who lived permanently at the Grand Hotel. He had stayed with the old lady, by name Mrs. Custance, for an hour or two during which they had tea and talked business. Mrs. Custance had known the late Charles Beringham and asked after his daughter.

'So unfortunate for that poor child,' she had said. 'What is becoming of her?'

Martin told her a little about Delia and her present difficulties. Mrs. Custance, a woman of means and without many living relations, took a sudden and violent interest in the girl who had been left so suddenly without a penny to face the world.

'I might be able to do something for her — and at any rate I would like to see her,' she had told Martin. 'I'm a lonely old woman and if it wouldn't bore her she might like to spend a few days here with me. It would do her good. You must ask her to come and talk it over.'

Martin thought this a tremendously good idea. But knowing Delia's independent spirit he could make no rash promises on her behalf. He was aware that he was a great favourite with the old lady and so, later in the day, did not hesitate to suggest that he should telephone Delia and ask her to come down and join them in Brighton for dinner.

'It's only an hour's run,' he said. 'And then I could take her back again. What do you think of the idea?'

The old lady was delighted. Martin put through the call to the Moderna Hotel. It was a considerable shock to him to hear from the manageress that Miss Beringham had left for good.

'But where has she gone?' Martin asked, with quickened heart-beats and an immediate sense of impending trouble.

'Abroad,' was the amazing answer.

Martin was staggered.

'Abroad!' he repeated. 'But do you mean she actually left London today?'

'I don't really know much about Miss Beringham,' came the huffy answer, 'except that she told me she was going on the night-boat from Newhaven to Dieppe.'

And without giving further information the lady rang off.

The lover in Martin Revell sprang to life very urgently. It was inevitable that he should remember the words she had spoken, lightly enough, in his office two weeks ago.

She had said foolish things about week-ends in Paris. Only *foolish* things of course. Delia would never behave in *that* fashion no matter how unhappy she was, nor how much she was tempted.

Then he glanced at his wrist-watch and a sudden thought struck him. The night-boat from Newhaven! He had on several occasions been on that boat, and it left about ten o'clock so far as he remembered. It was now getting on for six. Newhaven was only half an hour's car ride from Brighton. Since he was so near, why not hire a car, drive over to Newhaven and see Delia off? Not only would he have the pleasure of seeing her but of making quite certain that she was all right.

He reached Newhaven just after the arrival of the train from London. Leaving the car outside the station gates, he made his way through the wind and darkness to the boat, wondering as he did so if his informant at the Moderna had been right, and if he would really find Delia here, about to sail.

Then when he reached the dock and came alongside the boat he saw Delia and his heart gave a sudden and violent jerk. She was just at that precise moment stepping on board. He could not fail to recognise the charming figure in tweeds and beret. Neither could he help recognising the man just behind her. *Lingo Hewes!*

So this was the explanation of Delia's sudden and extraordinary decision to sail, tonight, to Dieppe. She was going with Lingo Hewes. *Delia and Hewes!* Martin's throat grew very dry and his teeth clenched.

Then an exclamation broke from him:

'No — by God — no!'

He wasn't going to stand by and see this done. Whether Delia acknowledged the fact or not, he, Martin, must constitute himself protector as well as friend.

He spoke to the policeman who was directing people on the wharf.

'Have I time to go on board and see a friend?'

'Yes, sir. About ten minutes. Hurry up.'

Martin hurried up the gangway on to the boat. Delia and Hewes were nowhere, now, to be seen. Martin searched the deck feverishly. He stopped a steward and spoke to him.

'I'm looking for a lady — a Miss Beringham — can you help me?'

'Most of the ladies have gone down to the saloon to lie down,' the man answered. 'It's going to be a rough crossing. I should inquire down there if I were you, sir.'

Martin turned and made his way down the stairs and found a stewardess.

'I want to speak to a Miss Beringham,' he said, and slipped half a crown into her hand. He knew the value of a tip when one was in a hurry. The woman smiled and nodded.

'We're full up — I'll just ask if there's anybody of that name.'

Delia had just at that moment taken off her shoes and her coat and settled herself on her bunk with a rug drawn up to her chin. Her eyes were closing wearily. She was very tired, her nerves were on edge and she wanted sleep.

The stewardess came up to her.

'Are you Miss Beringham?'

Delia opened her eyes and sat up.

'Yes.'

'A gentleman wants to speak to you. He's waiting just outside.'

Delia, without a thought of Martin in her head, curled her lip. Lingo, with his usual persistence, of course.

'Tell him I'm too ill to see anybody,' she said, and lay down again.

'It's a Mr. Revell,' said the stewardess, glancing at a card which Martin had given her.

Then Delia sat up again, much more alert, and pushed a dark lock of hair back from her forehead.

'Mr. Revell!' she repeated in a voice of astonishment.

'Yes, if you want to speak to him you'd better hurry. All friends will be going ashore in a moment.'

Delia slipped from her bunk, which was a top one, climbed down the little ladder, found her shoes and coat, and hurriedly combed back her hair. Martin here — but what on earth did he want and *how* on earth had he found out that she was crossing tonight?

She felt rather pleased at the thought that he was here and would bid her 'bon voyage'.

'Martin!' she exclaimed as she saw him outside the dormitory.

Had he been in a more receptive mood he would have heard the glad ring in her voice and seen a very real light of welcome in her eyes. But he was conscious only of acute anger and resentment when he looked at her.

'Where are you going?' he asked roughly and without greeting her. 'Why are you doing this?'

Taken aback, she stared at him.

'My *dear* Martin — '

'You've broken your word,' he interrupted, and anguished jealousy seemed to tear at his very heartstrings as he looked down at the charming young face with its cherry mouth and bright dark eyes and all the remembered sweetness and dearness of her.

'What on earth do you mean?'

'I asked you to give me your word that you would have nothing more to do with Hewes. You gave it and yet this is what happens — you're going to Dieppe with him! Delia — you're crazy — you can't be allowed to do it.'

For a moment his meaning was not

clear to her. Then she understood. Her own cheeks burned and she caught her breath.

'One moment — how do you know that I'm going to Dieppe with Lingo?'

'I saw you on board just now,' he said hotly. 'You won't deny that it was he who was with you?'

Her eyes narrowed.

'No, I won't deny that you saw me on board with Lingo. And I'm not going to trouble to deny that I'm going to Dieppe *with* him. If that's what you think — you can jolly well think it. And it ends our friendship, so far as *I'm* concerned.'

Bewildered and uncertain he looked down at her.

Some of his jealous anger was evaporating.

'Delia — ' he began.

But she turned and started to walk away from him. He caught her arm and pulled her back.

'Wait — please.'

She shook off his hand.

'I've nothing more to say to you, Martin.'

'But, Delia, you might at least explain — '

'I have nothing to explain. I was going to write from Dieppe and tell you everything. Now I don't think I'll even bother to do that. If you think I'm going to Dieppe with Lingo — well — you can't have much interest in me in the future. You don't like 'that kind of a girl', do you, Martin?'

'But look here — good lord — if I've been a fool I admit it — but I was so worried — '

He broke off, stammering. But she did not soften. She did not even begin to wonder why he should concern himself so vitally with her movements.

'All friends ashore, please!' sang out a stentorian voice. A bell clanged, and a long-drawn, dismal hoot issued from the funnel of the boat.

A feeling of panic seized Martin.

'Delia, I can't go until you've explained — my dear — and you must try to understand my anxiety for you — '

'You'd better go,' she broke in coldly, 'unless you want to find yourself crossing the Channel.'

'But, Delia — '

'Good-bye, Martin. And I think we'd better not see much more of each other. We don't get on very well, do we? You've gone to a lot of trouble on my behalf lately and for that I thank you, but please don't do any more for me. I'll manage my own affairs in future.'

'Delia!' he repeated, aghast.

'You'd better make haste, sir,' interrupted the stewardess, touching his arm.

'I'll write to you,' he stammered. 'This is all a mistake — we must never be anything but good friends — '

And then he turned and rushed up the stairs. He was only just in time. Another moment and the boat would have sailed.

It was by no means a happy Channel

crossing for Delia. It was the roughest one she had ever experienced and sleep was made impossible by the constant booming of the waves against the port-holes and the rocking and creaking of the ship, the whole way over. The heat was intolerable.

She was still sleepless and exhausted by the time they reached Dieppe — an hour late owing to the gale. Her head ached violently and she felt sick for the first time in her life.

She put on her coat and shoes and went out on deck. It was calm in the harbour here. With a slight feeling of pleasure she breathed in the night air, looked upon France again and considered that this was kind Melly's native town and that she would soon be with her old governess.

Somebody touched her on the shoulder.

She swung round and saw Lingo Hewes standing behind her, suitcase in his hand.

'Are you coming ashore?'

'No,' she said coldly.

'It was a pretty ghastly crossing.'

She made no answer but turned her head disdainfully from him.

'Look here,' she heard his slightly husky voice in her ear. 'Don't be huffy with me, old thing. It won't be much fun for you by yourself. Let me take care of you.'

'How exasperating you are,' she said. 'You can't ever see where you're not wanted.'

'Spending a holiday with Revell — our dear, worthy Martin, perhaps,' he sneered.

She made no reply but moved away from him, her hands thrust in her pockets, her head held high.

Hewes made no attempt to follow. He gave up the contest and moved off to catch the Paris express. He felt that Delia was the loser, after all. And since she was such a little idiot, let her get on with it!

Delia went back to the dormitory where the atmosphere was fresher and quieter now that it was almost empty and the portholes were open. She slept the sleep of exhaustion until eight o'clock.

She had never felt more anxious to see her former governess than on this August morning — a warm sunny morning which she felt was a happy augury — when at length she took a taxi from the docks to Rue St. Roche where Melly lived.

She was totally unprepared for the shock that awaited her when she reached the house of Madame Gaumet, Melly's married sister. She was received in a small parlour, ornately furnished in the French style, by a short, plump little Frenchman with large moustaches, who introduced himself to her as Monsieur Gaumet. He spoke in French which Delia understood.

It was a surprise to see her, he said. They had telegraphed to her last night. They had not dreamed that she was coming so soon nor that she would not receive their sad news.

Delia, with a sinking heart, questioned him quickly.

'What has happened? What is the bad news?'

Monsieur Gaumet pulled out a large pocket handkerchief and applied it to his eyes and his moustaches. With the extravagance and emotion of his race he explained that yesterday, very suddenly, his dear sister-in-law had died.

'You mean,' said Delia in a horrified voice, 'that *Mademoiselle Duplais* is dead?'

He said yes. He explained volubly. The *pauvre* Henriette had taken an excursion to Rouen with Madame Gaumet. It had been a hot day. She had a bad heart — perhaps that was already known to the young English lady — and she had dropped down in the street.

Delia, her face dead white, her eyes stricken, stared round the little parlour and then came back to Monsieur Gaumet who was still mopping his eyes, and divulging the beautiful qualities of

Henriette's character.

The shock of it numbed her. She sank into a chair and covered her face with her hands. She heard the little Frenchman's kind voice, sympathising with her in his flowery fashion.

She could see that she would not be able to remain with the Gaumets. And she did not really want to. They were strangers to her. She pulled herself together. She must go to a hotel for the moment, anyhow, and then decide what to do.

She pulled a note from her bag and pressed it into the little man's hand.

'Buy some flowers for her from me,' she said huskily, and rose to her feet.

It was not until she drove away from the little house along the sea-front that she fully realised what she had lost now that Melly was gone. This was a harrowing commencement to the life she had meant to lead in Dieppe with her old governess. Profoundly depressed and lonely she sat in the taxi and looked with sore eyes at the sparkling sea and the white buildings of the Casino.

The only hotel she knew of was the Metropole, wherein she had spent one night with her father a few years ago. The most expensive hotel in the place, of course, and they had had a magnificent private suite. No use going there. The Miss Beringham of today must find a cheap room and forget that she had ever occupied private suites!

She stopped the taxi and asked the driver's advice. He directed her to a small hotel, not far from the Casino, which he said would be clean, quite good, and not dear. So she was finally deposited there with her luggage, and found herself in a small back bedroom furnished in typical heavy French style; cheerless and rather gloomy.

She spent a lonely and depressing evening at the hotel and a still more depressing day followed it. Another twenty-four hours in Dieppe showed her conclusively that there was not the slightest chance of her getting a job out here. The only thing left for her to do was to return to London and make other plans.

★ ★ ★

When Delia boarded the boat for Newhaven she felt that her return was a little ignominious. But although she started out for England in a state of deep gloom, that short voyage was destined to mark a new and important epoch in Delia's career.

It bade fair to be a perfect crossing. At one o'clock, when the boat glided out of Dieppe Harbour, the sea was like a mill pond, the sky was blue and the sun shone radiantly. Delia settled herself in a deck chair, lay back and closed her eyes and let the warm sun beat on her face. This was better than being battered about in a gale — like the one in which she had sailed from Newhaven two nights ago.

She was aroused by a well-bred, rather attractive voice saying:

101

'I beg your pardon, but is this chair occupied?'

She opened her eyes and saw a very tall and broad-shouldered man in grey flannels, hall-marked British, standing beside an empty deck chair which was alongside her own.

'I don't think it belongs to anybody,' she replied. 'But I really don't know.'

'In that case I shall bag it,' he said.

She was conscious at once of liking him. She watched him through her lashes as he settled himself in the chair, took off his hat, and pulled out a packet of cigarettes. He was a man of over thirty, she judged, but he had the smile of a boy — delightfully spontaneous and disarming. He looked as though he had come back from the East. His face and hands were very brown. He was amazingly good-looking with light brown hair and the bluest eyes she had ever seen.

Silence for a few minutes and then — fate has a way of arranging these things — a gust of wind blew the paper which was lying on Delia's lap on to his own. He rescued it and handed it back with another of those gay and attractive smiles which made him look so youthful.

'Bit breezy, isn't it? — but gorgeous weather.'

'Thanks so much,' she murmured. 'Yes, it's gorgeous.'

'A pleasant change. I hear you've had a pretty dismal summer over here so far.'

'It has certainly rained persistently in England.'

'Good old England!' he laughed. 'What a climate! Yet one always goes back there as though it were the only place in the world. It has its points when compared with other countries.'

'Haven't you been in England lately?' she asked him.

'No. Just had three years in the Far East. Army — y'know. Back on leave — got off at Marseilles. Had a few days in Paris. Now I shall have six months' holiday I hope.'

'After three years in the Far East I expect you appreciate grey skies and the rain.'

He laughed.

'M'm — yes — but I like the sun. Were you on the Paris train? I didn't see you.'

'No, I've been in Dieppe for a couple of days.'

'Nothing to do, is there, except lose money at the tables?'

'That's all, I hate it.'

She was not very communicative.

'What's London like these days?' he asked her.

'Not as nice as it used to be,' she said, influenced by her own feelings. At one time she had adored London and life in Charles Street.

'Everybody seems hard up.'

Delia smiled.

'Yes — that's true enough.'

'There've been some fearful financial smashes — plenty of people are affected. A lot of fellows in the Regiment — men with private incomes

— have found themselves pretty short and had to cut down. Rather hard on the married ones. Of course I'm a bachelor and it doesn't matter quite so much to me, but I've dropped a good bit myself this year.'

'That's bad luck,' she murmured, and added under her breath: 'So have I!'

He gave her a humorous smile.

'Don't tell me that you gamble on the Stock Exchange! You look much too young for that.'

'No. But my father has died recently and left — nothing!'

She wondered why she was telling him about her private affairs after so short an acquaintance.

'It's awful tough luck on people who lose money through no fault of their own,' he said, in course of conversation. 'And these fellows — these big financiers like Kreuger who swindle a lot of small shareholders out of their money are the worst type of criminals. I used to have a fair bit of money in a company called the Empire Eastern. You may have heard of it.'

Delia did not answer but the colour suddenly ebbed from her cheeks and she sat still and straight, listening to him. He went on:

'The company smashed not so very long ago. I lost the lot — at least I don't believe we're going to get anything back. Another of those big financiers responsible for the disaster! Shot himself after the failure, and a good job — he's best out of it. It's a rotten stunt gambling with other folks' money. Beringham was the fellow's name. Do you remember the case?'

For a moment Delia did not answer. She felt physically sick. Without looking to the right or the left of her, in a stifled voice she said:

'Don't judge Charles Beringham — too harshly. It may not have been his fault.'

'Of course it was, and what annoys me is that these fellows generally have a nice little nest-egg stowed away for their own families in case of disaster — ' began her companion hotly, and then seemed suddenly aware of her distress.

'Have I said anything to upset you?' he added anxiously.

For an instant shame bit into her like an acid and then she turned and looked straight at him with a proud gesture of the head. She was not going to be ashamed of Daddy. She said:

'My name is Delia Beringham. I'm Charles Beringham's daughter.'

It was the man's turn to colour furiously. An exclamation broke from him:

'I say — I'm most awfully sorry — I didn't realise — I say, what must you think of me? How frightfully indiscreet of me — I do apologise! I must have hurt you and I wouldn't have done that for the world — ' He broke off, stammering.

Delia felt sorry for him. After all, if he had suffered through the failure of the company he had a right to feel resentful.

'Do forgive me,' he begged. 'I'm really more sorry than I can say.'

'Don't worry,' she said. 'I quite understand, and you have a right to say what you think.'

'No right to say it to you.'

'How could you know who I was?'

'I didn't know, but I oughtn't to have said anything — '

'That's nonsense.'

'Anyhow, I shall never forgive myself for uttering one word about your father.'

She swallowed hard and gripped the side of her deck chair with two small, hot hands.

'I just don't want you to blame him altogether,' she said. 'I think he must have had a very bad time before he died — Martin — our solicitor — told me how harassed he had been and how hard he had tried to put things right.'

'I'm sure of that.'

'It's only natural that you should feel sore when you've lost your money through him.'

'I've only lost some of it — I've

108

plenty left — I can't tell you how much I wish I'd never mentioned it.'

She smiled at him again, and some of her own shame and pain died away. He was really rather a dear, and pathetically anxious to make amends for his indiscretion.

'I just want to tell you one thing,' she said gently. 'You said something just now about 'the nest-egg' that these financiers put away for their families. Well, that isn't so in Daddy's case. He left me with nothing — nothing at all. All his estates and possessions have been sold to pay his debts. I went over to Dieppe two days ago to try and get a job. I couldn't get one so I'm going back to London to look for something else. I thought I'd just tell you that, anyhow.'

The man's brown face was still burning with embarrassment. He said huskily:

'I'm most awfully sorry about it all. I want you to tell me that you'll forget what I said and be friends with me. I'd be frightfully honoured if you'd accept my friendship, anyhow.'

Tears sprang to her eyes. She blinked them back and tried to smile.

'That's nice of you.'

'Then you will?' he asked eagerly. 'Will you allow me to see you again when we're back in town?'

'I don't suppose we'll come across each other very often. I've got to settle down to hard work and I expect you'll be very busy enjoying your leave.'

'I shan't consider that it's been a decent leave unless I do see something of you,' he said, with that boyish enthusiasm which she could not help liking.

'Do you live in London?'

'I live nowhere in particular. I'm in the Guards — a Regular. I spend my leave with one or two relations — aunts and cousins and friends. My parents are not alive. I generally make London my headquarters, so please allow me to ring you up sometime and suggest a meeting.'

'It's very nice of you,' she said.

'It's terribly nice of you to forgive me,' he stammered.

'There wasn't anything to forgive. I think it rather magnanimous of you to offer your friendship to the daughter of — '

'Look here,' he interrupted. 'We certainly shan't be friends if you try and say things like that. I'm proud and honoured to know you. You're being marvellous and I know you must be having a pretty tough time of it.'

'Don't ever pity me!' she flashed. 'I shall be all right and I'm going to make something out of my life — you'll see!'

'But you're so young — '

'Not so young that I can't take care of myself,' she said impatiently. 'I shall be twenty-one at the end of this year.'

'Good lord — that *is* young. Do you know I'm thirty-four?'

'Do you know you haven't even told me your name yet?' she laughed.

'It's Radleigh. William Radleigh, commonly called 'Bill' — Captain, to give me my full title.'

'Thanks. You know my name.'

'Yes,' he said, a trifle awkwardly, then added on a bright note: 'Look here — will you dine with me in town tonight?'

'I don't think I'd better.'

'Are you otherwise engaged?'

'No.'

'Well, neither am I. And I've got nothing fixed except one or two visits to relations and friends for next week. I always stay at Brown's when I'm on leave. I shall go straight there. Where shall I find you?'

'I don't know where I'm going yet.'

'But haven't you anywhere — I mean you can't be absolutely on your own!' he stammered.

'But I am. I'm singularly short of relations. And I haven't very many friends who mean anything. People change so, you know, when you're on the rocks.'

'But you can't be on the rocks!' he protested.

She laughed a little. His blue eyes were so horrified and he seemed so genuinely concerned for her.

She gave him a little more information about her present position; told him about Martin Revell and Betty Willis.

'Is this solicitor fellow a good pal to you?' Radleigh asked her.

She answered that question a trifle evasively.

'I hate to think of you absolutely alone and without prospects,' Bill Radleigh said after a while. 'It doesn't seem right.'

'Oh, something will turn up,' she said lightly.

'Well, you will dine with me tonight, won't you? It will cheer us both up.'

She surrendered.

'I'd like to dine with you,' she said. 'You are sure you have nothing else to do?'

'I can think of nothing that I'd like to do so much,' he assured her.

During the rest of that journey to

Newhaven the new friendship was consolidated. They were together until they reached Victoria and there took separate taxis. Radleigh had a good deal of luggage. He apologised for not driving her to her destination.

'That's quite all right,' she said, smiling.

'Can you meet me about eight o'clock?'

'Yes,' she nodded.

'Let's say the Café Royal. I have a weakness for the old place — I always go there the first night I'm home on leave.'

'It's all been rebuilt and redecorated while you were abroad.'

'Well, let's go and study the change.'

'Right!'

He put her in a taxi and the driver took her cabin trunk and suitcase.

'Where shall I tell him?' asked Radleigh.

'I honestly don't know,' she said, and burst out laughing.

But Bill did not laugh. He loved this

child for her courage, but he could not bear to think of her solitary state.

'Look here,' he groaned, 'this is all wrong — '

'Don't be absurd,' she said lightly, and added stoutly: 'As a matter of fact I *do* know where I want to go. The Moderna, just off Dorset Square.'

'Is that a good place?'

'Highly respectable for a young girl alone,' she laughed.

He had to laugh with her now. But after the taxi had driven her away he stood looking after her with a very serious expression in his blue and handsome eyes.

Bill Radleigh for the first time in his thirty-four years was in love — hopelessly in love with a girl whom he had only known for four hours, and the daughter of the man whose failure had reduced the Radleigh income by at least a third!

And Delia, her spirits higher than they had been since her brief, harrowing sojourn in Dieppe, returned to the Moderna Hotel. She had never intended to return there. She hated everything about it. But she knew it and she could put up with it for the present until she had more definite plans for the future. Meanwhile she had made a new and good friend in Bill Radleigh, which was a comforting thought.

She began to look forward to her dinner with him tonight.

★　★　★

Martin came down to breakfast both looking and feeling depressed.

During the forty-eight hours which had elapsed since his disastrous interview with Delia, on that stormy night at Newhaven, he had been quite unable to get her out of his mind.

When he found a letter with a French postage-stamp and addressed in Delia's handwriting, awaiting him, his heart leaped in his breast and he flushed to the eyes like a boy. He murmured a

116

greeting to his aunt, shot a brief 'good morning' at Elinor who sat opposite him, and then eagerly ripped open the envelope.

Mrs. Warnleigh and her adopted daughter exchanged significant glances.

If there was one person in the world whom Eva Warnleigh loved it was Martin. She had adored him when he was a small, rather grave, shy little boy with flashes of humour and a most affectionate disposition. He still seemed to her without fault and she still adored him. He had always been extraordinarily sweet and kind to her.

But Elinor, she knew, had different feelings. The poor girl had long ago ceased to regard Martin as an adopted brother. She loved him hopelessly — Mrs. Warnleigh was quite certain it was hopeless because, although Elinor was a dear and Mrs. Warnleigh was devoted to her, she was not the type of woman to attract Martin.

Elinor sat quietly eating her breakfast, but kept her solemn blue eyes fixed upon the young man opposite her. Then Martin spoke.

'This is from Delia.'

'Yes, dear?' said Mrs. Warnleigh, with a slight twinkle in her eyes.

Martin bent over his plate of bacon and eggs. His cheeks were red.

'What is she doing?' asked Elinor.

'I don't know,' muttered Martin. 'She doesn't say — just gives her new address.'

'Humph!' said Elinor, and shrugged her shoulders.

Martin made a poor breakfast. The curtness of Delia's note had hurt him badly.

'I hope the child will be all right,' remarked Mrs. Warnleigh. 'I don't really approve of young girls rushing about the Continent alone. She's such an independent little thing.'

'Yes,' said Martin gloomily.

'By the way,' said Mrs. Warnleigh, changing the subject brightly, 'you haven't forgotten that it's Elinor's birthday today, have you, Martin?'

He looked up quickly.

'Oh, I say, I'm sorry, Elinor — how remiss of me not to have wished you many happy returns! I've got a little parcel for you up in my room, as a matter of fact.'

She flushed with pleasure. With that colour in her cheeks and light in her eyes she looked quite attractive. But Martin, although he was fond of Elinor — she had always been very nice to him — had no very real interest in her. She was a little too dull and dowdy. He pushed back his chair, went upstairs and fetched her present for her. A beautiful edition of Masefield's poems which she had wanted.

'It's perfectly lovely — thanks awfully, Martin!' exclaimed Elinor, and pored over her treasure. 'You must write in it for me.'

'Yes,' said Martin vaguely.

'How about a little dinner to celebrate this evening,' suggested Mrs. Warnleigh. 'That's what we did last year.'

'It would be lovely,' said Elinor, with unusual animation. The thought of dining with Martin in public always excited her.

'Certainly,' said Martin, not caring what he did. 'Anything you suggest.'

'Last year we went to the Café Royal,' said his aunt. 'One gets a very good dinner there, and I hear it's just been done up. Shall we go there?'

'It will be great fun,' said Martin, with an effort.

But his mind was haunted by the thought of Delia when he went down to his office that day.

He was in no festive mood when finally he got back to Hampstead that night and changed into his dinner-jacket.

But Elinor was in a state of terrific excitement and quite unlike her calm and retiring self. Her adopted mother had most tactfully retired to bed with a headache.

'I've got a cold coming, my dear, and if you and Martin will forgive me I won't go out tonight,' she said. 'You two young people run along and have a nice little celebration dinner by yourselves.'

When Martin heard that his aunt was not coming, he remained indifferent. He was so harassed about Delia that he did not mind whether he dined alone with Elinor, or in a crowd. But he was momentarily roused from his apathy when he came down to the drawing-room and saw the Elinor who awaited him. There was some extraordinary change in her which for a moment bewildered him. He stood staring at her, frowning, and she looked back, cheeks on fire, heart pounding, wondering what impression she was making.

Then he realised two things. First of all she had had her hair cut short and secondly that she was quite smartly dressed. It was a transformation from the rather old-fashioned Elinor with her bun of hair, and she looked years younger and — he admitted it — quite pretty.

As they drove off in a taxi to Regent

Street, Martin said:

'I shall have to keep an eye on you tonight, Elinor. You look about twenty and that dress is most effective.'

Her pulses stirred.

'I'm glad you like it. But you needn't think that I — '

'What?'

'That I take any interest in other men,' she stammered.

'Well, you ought to,' he laughed. 'It's quite time you thought about marrying, my dear old girl.'

She did not answer that.

They were half-way through a friendly and pleasant meal at the Café Royal when something happened to rouse Martin thoroughly from his state of depression.

A man and a girl entered the restaurant, preceded by the head waiter, who with beckoning hand led them to a table at the other end of the room.

Martin looked at the girl as she passed and then an exclamation broke from him. He rose to his feet.

'Good God! *Delia!*'

Elinor followed his gaze and she, too, saw the familiar figure of Delia Beringham. Delia looking lovely and distinctive as usual in a long green dress of some silky, shimmering material with a short green velvet coat to match. Delia, perfectly turned out from her smooth dark head to the tips of her small green slippers, and beside her a tall man with light blue eyes set in a very brown, handsome face.

She did not notice Martin. She walked with that light, graceful carriage so familiar to him, straight to her table. Martin sat down again, breathing heavily.

Elinor, feeling that her whole evening was spoilt by this sudden intrusion of Delia Beringham's presence, stole a look at Martin's face.

'I thought Delia was in France,' she said.

'So did I.'

'Who's the man?'

'I haven't the slightest idea.'

'Are you going to speak to her?'

'Yes,' said Martin suddenly, between his teeth, and stood up. 'If you'll forgive me just a moment, Elinor.'

She would have forgiven him anything, but she felt sore and disappointed as she watched him cross the restaurant to the table at which Delia and her companion had seated themselves.

Delia had come out to enjoy herself. She had been through a harrowing time, and she decided to extract what she could in the way of harmless amusement from this evening's entertainment. Bill Radleigh was a charming companion and she had not been blind to the warm admiration which had leaped into his eyes when he met her.

'You can't imagine how marvellous it is to come back from old India and find a perfect August night in London, and a perfect girl to have dinner with,' had been his greeting to her.

'We'll go and dance somewhere

after,' Bill suggested, as they sat down at their table. 'Would you like that?'

'I adore dancing,' she said.

'Then we must do a lot of it.'

She smiled and shook her head at him.

'This child won't have much time for dancing. She's got to work!'

Radleigh had no time to reply. Martin came up to their table and said:

'Delia!'

Bill rose to his feet. Delia flushed to the roots of her hair.

'Martin!' she exclaimed, in an astonished voice.

Bill thought:

'Ah! This is the lawyer fellow. Looks rather a nice chap.'

But Delia had no smile for Martin. She looked up at him coldly.

'I didn't expect to see you here.'

'I — I didn't expect to see you,' he stammered. 'We're celebrating Elinor's birthday.'

'Oh, yes,' said Delia. 'May I introduce you — Captain Radleigh — Mr.

Revell, my solicitor.'

Martin and Bill shook hands and exchanged formal greetings. Martin bent a little over Delia's chair.

'I'd like to see you sometime,' he said, in a low voice. 'I thought you were still in Dieppe — I'm rather surprised — '

'I came back this morning,' she said, in the same cold voice. 'I'll come round to the office tomorrow. I want to talk business.'

That was scarcely encouraging but it was all that Martin could extract from her. While this man, Radleigh, was with her, he could scarcely pursue an intimate discussion. So perforce, he said:

'I shall be in all the morning. Come when you like. Au revoir.'

'Remember me to Elinor,' said Delia politely.

The two men bowed to each other and Martin went back to his own table.

'So that's the lawyer, eh?' said Bill Radleigh, regaining his chair. 'He's got a clever face. Full of brains, I imagine.'

'Yes — Martin is quite clever.'

And that was all that Delia had to say about him.

The rest of the evening was a decided success. Bill was charming to her and as enthusiastic as a boy about his leave and this 'first night back in the old country'.

They went on to a revue — it was half over when they got there, but that did not seem to matter. And after that they had supper and danced at Malmaison.

In the taxi, when he was driving her back to her hotel, he begged her to meet him again.

'We weren't meant to meet on the boat this morning just for nothing. I believe in destiny,' he said. 'And I'm quite sure fate meant us to be pals, Delia. We had such a strange introduction — and I shan't be happy until I've lived down the things I said to you.'

'They're all forgotten, Bill,' she said. 'And you needn't worry about them any more.'

'But I'm a little anxious about you. You've been sweet and gay and brave, but under it all you're damned miserable, aren't you?'

'No — not at all,' she protested, and tilted her head.

'Well, then, I *shall* be unless you'll come out with me again tomorrow!' he exclaimed.

'Very well, I'll come.'

'Tomorrow?'

'No, I must look for work tomorrow — ' Then she remembered Martin and added, laughing: 'And I've got to see my solicitor, too. He's pawning my car and my jewels for me — '

Bill said nothing. He was learning not to sympathise with Delia. She hated it so.

'I can get you on the phone at Brown's, can't I?' she asked him.

'Yes. And leave a message if I'm not in.'

'I'll do that, then.'

'Promise to ring me up soon.'

'I will, and thanks awfully, Bill.'

The taxi stopped outside Delia's hotel. She grimaced as she saw it. She must certainly find more attractive lodgings.

She was altogether touched when Radleigh lifted her hand to his lips with a gesture of homage.

'Good night — nicest and bravest girl I've ever met,' he said.

That was the end of their evening, and it seemed to Delia a very nice ending, too.

★ ★ ★

That next morning Delia received a summons from the Employment Agency near Victoria Street to which she had applied some time ago. They intimated that they had an opening which they thought 'might interest her'.

Delia, extremely tired after her late evening with Bill, read her letter with one eye open but as soon as she reached the end of it, the other eye opened and she sprang quickly from her bed and dressed.

Almost as soon as the office in Victoria Street opened she was there, eager to see what was being offered her.

The gaunt female with spectacles, who had first interviewed Delia, gave her a hearing now. She regarded her suspiciously. Delia did not know quite what she suspected but was aware that the woman had some doubts about her capabilities, if not her character.

'Of course you have no experience,' she said, looking over the rim of her glasses at the charming young figure which seemed to her much too attractive and well-dressed. 'But They said when I told Them about you that They would give you a chance.'

Delia's eyes twinkled.

'Who are They?'

'The Kosihome Carpet-Sweeper Company.'

Delia swallowed hard.

'What do they want? A cook or a companion-help?'

The gaunt female bridled. She had

no sense of humour.

'A saleswoman, Miss Beringham,' she said stiffly.

Delia gripped her bag tightly. Her brow puckered.

'A saleswoman! Good lord, I've never tried to sell anything — except a few of my own clothes and I believe I was swindled over those.'

The female sniffed. 'Of course if you don't wish to give it a trial — '

'Oh, yes — indeed I will,' put in Delia quickly, realising that she was not being a very good advocate for herself.

The woman licked a finger, turned over the pages of a large ledger, ran a bony finger down several lines and came to a full-stop. She continued to eye Delia suspiciously.

'Well, here it is — Mr. Brown, general manager of the Kosihome Company was here yesterday. We have recently supplied him with two sales-women. They are doing very nicely and he wants another. I mentioned your name and he said he would like a young lady of good appearance.

Again Delia swallowed to conceal her mirth. She wished Bill Radleigh were here. He would have enjoyed this. She wondered if she would be considered of 'good appearance' by Mr. Brown.

'What do I have to do?' she asked.

'Travel with this sweeper which is in a nice little case and get what orders you can. You work on a small salary and commission. And of course it depends on your own efforts how much you earn.'

A little of Delia's humour evaporated. A commercial traveller! How the mighty had fallen.

'Well — would you care to call on Mr. Brown?' a chilly voice broke in upon her thoughts.

'Yes,' said Delia promptly. 'If you have absolutely nothing else on your books.'

'Nothing suitable. You said you can't cook and you've no experience with children and I haven't had any inquiries for a chauffeuse.'

'Then I'll see Mr. Brown.'

The woman handed the letter to Delia.

'Here's the address.'

Delia looked at it. *H. S. Brown. Kosihome Carpet-Sweeper Company, Ream Street, S.W.1.*

'It's just off Victoria Street,' she was told. 'Not far from this office down the Westminster end.'

Delia emerged from the Employment Agency into the sunshine and walked thoughtfully towards Ream Street. About an hour later she presented herself at the office of Revell & Revell. A rather flushed Delia with small dark head held high and lips set in a determined line. She carried in her right hand a long leather suitcase of peculiar shape, the weight of which seemed a little heavy for her. She was in a good humour despite any qualms she may have secretly entertained about her new and rather undignified status, as she walked into Martin's room. But he — the usually calm, sane lawyer — was in a state of nervous tension when he received her. He was pale and his hands were shaking. He was just a man badly in love and loving without hope.

He held out a hand dumbly. She smiled and set her case with a thud on the floor. She had no knowledge of his suffering — no instinct about it. She was the old, gay, *insouciante* Delia who used to laugh at him, tease him, pass him by with just a touch of gossamer wings like a charming butterfly which vanished almost as soon as it delighted his vision.

'Good morning,' she said briskly, 'I've called on behalf of the Kosihome Electric Carpet-Sweeper Company.'

Martin blinked and stared.

'What the — ' he began.

'Oh please give me a trial,' she interrupted with a charming and beseeching smile. 'I won't keep you a moment. If you would just let me demonstrate our wonderful machine — show you what a difference it will make on a piece of your nice rug here — '

She stooped and began to open the suitcase.

Martin, flabbergasted, stared at the bent head with its small straw hat which had an impudent bunch of flowers just under the brim. Although simple, it suggested that Miss Beringham still possessed extravagant clothes.

'Delia, what is all this about?' he began again.

She had opened the case and was fixing together some instrument which he now could see was an electrical sweeper, and raised a pink, determined young face.

'I assure you when you have tested this splendid sweeper, you will never want to use anything else,' she exclaimed.

Now Martin, on an ordinary occasion, would have entered into the spirit of this and enjoyed it. But it must be remembered that he was in that unhappy and slightly deranged condition which people call 'love' and he had scarcely slept all night. He was not in the best state to appreciate any kind of joke. He snapped at her:

'What the devil is all this?'

Delia produced the carpet-sweeper, and stood up, proud and still smiling.

'I'm sorry I haven't a card — I've got to have some printed. But I'm the representative of the 'Kosihome — ' '

'You've said all that before,' broke in Martin.

Delia shrugged her shoulders. She had entered the office in good spirits and quite prepared to be friendly with Martin.

'Oh well — the joke's over,' she said. 'I just thought I'd try my best saleswoman-manner on you.' She began to take the sweeper to pieces and place them back in the case, and added: 'This is my new job.'

Somewhat mollified, Martin received this piece of news.

'Your new job?'

'Yes — I only got it twenty minutes ago. I've just been to see a terrifying gentleman from the North with a strong Lancashire accent, who calls himself Mr. Brown. He engaged me as a traveller for the firm. I'm to make a tour of south-east London. I shall get ten pounds a week, my travelling expenses, and a commission of ten per cent on every sweeper sold. The sweeper being twenty-eight pounds in value, it depends on how many I sell how much I earn. Mr. Brown tells me that I might make fifteen or sixteen pounds a week if I am lucky. On the other hand I might make nothing over and above my salary, in which case I should soon get the sack.'

Martin pulled up a chair for her and handed her a cigarette. His heart was beating faster than usual but he preserved a calm exterior.

'So that's it,' he said.

'Isn't it marvellous?' she said with a brief laugh. 'Delia as a commercial traveller!'

'I think it's the most ridiculous thing I've ever heard of.'

The bright, dark almond-shaped eyes opened wide at him.

'But why? It's perfectly respectable work. You're not going to give me a little lecture, are you, Martin, and tell me it isn't nice for a young girl?'

He flushed up to the eyes and winced under the sarcasm.

'Do I strike you as being nothing but an insufferable prig?'

She was a little surprised at the undercurrent of feeling in his voice, gave him a quick look, then took a whiff of her cigarette. Martin was very touchy these days.

'Well, it *is* quite an honest job and quite a safe one for a poor lone girl.'

'I dare say. But I don't think it's suitable for you.'

'Beggars can't be choosers,' she brought out the old axiom.

His irritation vanished. There was something so magical about Delia's personality, and he could not fail to recognise her pluck.

'My dear, I hope it will be all right.

As long as you're all right, nothing else matters.'

Her eyes softened.

'I shall be all right — don't take me and my doings so seriously, Martin.'

'I — they are serious — to me!' he stammered.

'You worry too much.'

'You can hardly expect me to appreciate the thought of you selling from door to door.'

'It's got a funny side.'

'And a heart-breaking side too. People will be rude to you — you won't find it easy — and you may sell nothing. And it's horribly tiring too. That case is much too heavy for you — ' He picked it up and weighed it in his hand — 'Much too heavy,' he repeated. 'And ten pounds a week — why, you can barely live on it.'

'No, but I hope to sell one or two sweepers and I've still got a little capital to draw on for necessities. By the way — what about my car?'

'Still in the market. But we'll find a

decent buyer if we bide our time.'

'Thanks,' she said.

Their eyes met. The memory of Lingo Hewes and the scene on the Channel steamer sprang to life between them.

For the first time, Delia took close stock of Martin and noticed his pallor and uneasiness. He was looking rather ill.

'Aren't you fit, Martin?' she asked quite kindly.

'Quite, thanks.'

He came and stood in front of her again.

'I owe you an apology — ' he began.

'Oh that's all right,' she broke in. 'You were a complete idiot that night and really rather insulting to me — I was frightfully angry — but we'll forget about it.'

He felt an agony of longing to make fuller explanation.

'You see — I — when I saw you on that boat with that swine — '

'You needn't go into details,' she

140

broke in again, 'I tell you I'll forget about it.'

He persisted. 'But it was damnable of me to have even suggested — oh, hang it — you had every right to be angry, but I was just worried to death about you — that's all.'

'My dear Martin, I keep telling you not to worry about me.'

He gave a short, unhappy laugh.

'I'll have to try not to, I can see.'

She knitted her brows.

'I've got to lead my own life — I know you're my friend — that you were Daddy's friend — but under the circumstances I must choose for myself.'

He turned his face from her.

'Yes.'

'And even if I had been going away with Lingo — I don't see what you could have done about it, or what right you would have had to interfere.'

His head swung round to her again and she was suddenly startled at the sight of his face. It was a mask of suffering.

'No right to interfere, perhaps,' he said hoarsely. 'But if you imagine I would let you do a thing like that — with a fellow like that — without making some effort to stop you — I may have no right to interfere — but good God, I couldn't stand that.' He broke off, moving his head from side to side as though he were tormented.

Martin's expression and his sudden loss of control reduced Delia to speechlessness.

Martin recovered himself.

'But of course, as you say, I've been a fool — you wouldn't do such a thing,' he said in a calmer tone.

For him the dangerous moment had passed. He did not realise how far he had given himself away. But Delia's face was burning.

'Well, we needn't get all worked up about it,' she murmured. 'I daresay it did look very suspicious, but Lingo's presence on that boat was as much of a surprise to me as it was to you. And he was the last person I wanted to meet. I told you I'd finished with him and I meant it. I was going over to Dieppe to my old governess, Melly — Mademoiselle Duplais. Perhaps you remember her?'

'I think she had just left when I first met you.'

'Well, I was going to stay with her and get a job out in France.'

'I see,' said Martin in a low voice, and thought, gloomily: 'I have made a sanguinary idiot of myself!'

'When I got to Dieppe I found that poor Melly had died of heart failure in Rouen,' Delia added with a tremor in her voice.

'Died!' he repeated.

'Yes. It was awful. Such a shock.'

'My dear, how rotten for you!'

She tilted her head and tightened her lips.

'I'm getting used to shocks. There was no use staying out there — it didn't seem easy to get nice work — so I came straight back and on board I ran up against Captain Radleigh — Bill!'

'I see.'

Martin was learning not to show his jealousy even if he felt it.

Delia told him the history of her first meeting with Radleigh.

'It was so terribly awkward for him, poor man, saying those awful things about Daddy and not realising that I was his daughter,' she ended. 'I had to be sorry for him and he's frightfully nice and kind.' Then she added quickly in a changed tone: 'Martin, you never told me that so many people lost money when the Empire Eastern Company smashed.'

Martin busied himself with a cigarette.

'What was the use of worrying you with all the wretched details?'

'But are many people ruined through Daddy?'

'There was nothing criminal about it — no fraud — he was absolutely honest as daylight. You need never think otherwise, Delia, but it was just bad luck. Another and bigger concern smashed the Empire Eastern, and after that crash there were others and it ruined him.'

'I understand.'

Her lips were quivering now and her eyes were full of tears. He went quickly to her side. He had to exercise all his control in order not to gather her up in his arms, at that moment.

'My dear, don't think about it — please!'

Awkwardly she got up and moved away from Martin. She made herself speak lightly again:

'Well, I'd better take myself off, hadn't I? I've got to start on my travels at once. I'm going to Upper Norwood this afternoon for a beginning.'

He gave her a yearning look.

'You have all my admiration.'

'That's a change from you, Martin.'

His cheeks coloured. She hastened to add: 'As a matter of fact you've always been frightfully decent to me — I'm really very grateful.'

'You do understand about the boat — '

'Yes.'

She understood so much more than he guessed.

She offered Martin her hand with a gesture of friendliness so rare on her part that he was shaken by it. He crushed her fingers tightly.

'I take back everything I've ever said about you being a frivolous member of society,' he said. 'I think you're wonderful!'

3

September was the warmest month of the year. After a summer which had been fine by fits and starts, the early autumn came in like a brilliant August.

A year ago Delia would have adored the heat — revelled in it. But this year the heat was far from welcome. Under present circumstances it merely intensified the discomforts of her existence.

She was, after three weeks, still 'travelling' for the Kosihome Carpet-Sweeper Company. That meant trudging from door to door hour after hour, carrying that heavy case. It meant blistered feet and an aching body and spirits flagging, despite strenuous efforts to keep them aloft. It had ceased to be a joke, this job of trying to earn a living by selling an article on the commission basis!

Delia had learned to expect disappointment and rebuffs, nevertheless she felt every disappointment keenly when it came.

It was not easy to exist on her salary. The necessity for selling sweepers regularly was a very real one. At the end of the long, tiring days — she had never in her life before known what it was to be so tired and dispirited — she was sometimes tempted to give up the job. But pride stepped in and prevented her from surrendering.

Life had its compensations. There was for instance an almost ridiculous amount of pleasure to be extracted from putting through a sale. Moments of triumph in her job seemed worth all the slogging and difficulties. Then there were week-ends when friends like Betty Willis and Martin and Bill Radleigh showered her with devotion. Now and then on a Saturday or Sunday, Betty came in her car and took Delia out of town into the country. Her loyalty to Delia remained unshaken.

Delia had moved, three weeks ago, from the Moderna to a small furnished bed-sitting-room off Bayswater Road. It was only a cheap back room with attendance but it was clean and she could cook on a gas ring. She preferred that to being one of a ghastly crowd in an odious boarding-house.

The bed-sitting-room was now her home. She had tried to make it look nice with one or two things saved from the wreckage. A beautiful piece of blue glass; a gay china bowl; a pair of brocade curtains; some books and a photograph of her mother in her wedding dress. A framed water-colour of Spain which she had bought in Malaga hung where she could see it when she lay in bed.

Betty had insisted on giving her a big satin cushion and a charming green and silver spread for the bed. Martin had sent her a Persian rug to cover the shabby hair-carpet. And everywhere there were flowers. Those came from Bill. Carnations, roses, chrysanthemums, bronze and yellow and pink — great masses of them sent from a florist's every other day. He was incorrigible. All these things transformed the shabby bed-sitting-room and made it attractive so that Delia need no longer be depressed by her surroundings.

But this afternoon when Delia got back from that exhausting day in Dulwich, she felt that all her courage was fast deserting her.

When Jenny, the daily looked in, Delia was lying full length on the bed with both eyes shut and her hands pressed to her hot, throbbing temples.

'Want anything?'

'Yes. Tea — badly, Jenny,' said Delia.

'I'll make you a cuppa,' said Jenny, who adored this young and beautiful lodger who had made her bedroom look what Jenny called 'like on the picshures!' 'My! You do look pale! Ain't you 'ad no luck with that there sweeper?'

'Not today, Jenny,' said Delia with a faint smile.

'What a shime! An' this weather so crool 'ard on your feet.'

The sympathy of the little Cockney brought the rare tears to Delia's eyes.

When Jenny had brought the tea — an unusual treat — Delia drained two cups thirstily but could not eat. She was too tired.

She was supposed to be going out to dinner and a theatre with Martin tonight. What she really wanted to do was to get into bed and sleep. On the other hand she supposed it would do her good to get out and she did not like to turn down the appointment, especially as Martin had taken seats for a new play.

At half-past six, however, she was still so tired that she was on the verge of tears, and the climax came when she tried to put on a satin evening shoe and found it impossible. Those slim white feet of hers, which had always been so carefully tended by Marie, were swollen, blistered, inflamed. She managed to squeeze on one shoe but the pain was so excruciating that she kicked it off again at once.

That settled it. She would have to ring up Martin and tell him she was not well enough to go out with him tonight.

There was a telephone in the hall, just outside her bed-sitting-room, and she put her coins in the slot and called through to Martin's house in Hampstead.

'Don't say you're not coming!' were his first words.

'Well, I don't think I can, Martin. I really don't feel fit enough.'

'My dear!' His voice was immediately full of concern. 'What's wrong?'

She found herself laughing rather hysterically.

'Got a bad foot — that's all.'

'What's happened?'

'Oh, nothing much.' She was trying so hard to be nonchalant, not to let him know the real cause of those blistered toes and swollen ankles.

Martin, however, was not easily put off.

'I shall get straight into a car and come round and see you,' he said.

'Oh, don't — ' began Delia weakly.

But Martin had rung off.

Half an hour later he was in her bed-sitting-room, sitting on the arm of a chair talking to her while she, in the one black and gold cocktail suit which had not been sold, curled up on top of her divan bed, smoked a cigarette and tried to make light of her troubles.

'It's just that I'm frightfully tired out, I think, Martin,' she said. 'But there isn't the slightest need to worry about me.'

'It's that rotten job,' he said, scowling.

'I don't mind it. And last week I made quite a lot on commission. It's just this heat which is trying. It's so unusual for the time of year, isn't it?'

He looked at the pale young face and found it much too tired and thin for his liking.

'Delia, my dear, I wish I could see

something else ahead for you — something other than this!' he said earnestly. 'I don't want you to crack up.'

'I shan't do that — I'm much too young and strong.'

'But it isn't like you to feel too tired to come out and do a show.'

She curled the offending feet well under her.

'I just want a long night's rest. You do understand, don't you, Martin?'

'Of course, my dear.'

'I'm so sorry — I know you've got tickets — can you take somebody else — '

'I don't want to take anybody else,' he said with a charming smile which lit up his serious face.

'Why not take Elinor?' she suggested.

Martin frowned and looked at his cigarette.

'I don't think I wish to.'

'Hasn't she got a crush on you, Martin?' Delia asked a little wickedly.

He flushed self-consciously.

'I think Elinor would make a good

wife,' observed Delia.

'If you are suggesting her as a possible wife for me, get it right out of your head,' said Martin abruptly. 'I've known Elinor much too long and too well to entertain any feeling of that sort for her.'

'I'm sure it's time you got married, Martin.'

At that crucial moment Martin was longing to say:

'I love you — I would get married tomorrow if you would have me — I've loved you for so long! There can never be anybody else — '

But the old reserve and caution were too strong for him. He conquered the desire to turn around and pour out his feelings, and said in a casual voice:

'I'm quite happy as I am, and I don't think I shall ever marry now.'

Delia, silent a moment, played idly with a box of matches. She was wondering if that answer disappointed her — if she had wanted anything more from him than that. Then she inwardly jeered at herself. She was not getting sentimental about Martin — Martin of all men in the world — how absolutely idiotic! He was a confirmed bachelor — always had been. He was not in the least in love with her. She had made a mistake about that. She spoke to him gaily:

'I don't think I shall ever marry, either, Martin.'

He forced himself to face her, then, and to be as cheerful as she was on the subject.

'Oh, but I'm sure you will. Why, you absurd child, talking about being an old maid when you're scarcely twenty-one.'

'Do you realise that it's my coming of age next week?'

'Good lord! Is it really?' he asked with a sense of shock.

'Yes. One generally has a twenty-first birthday party, doesn't one?'

The sweet red under-lip trembled a little, but Delia smiled and shook back a dark curve of hair which had fallen across her eyes. 'Well — I'll give one

— if my landlady doesn't have a fit, I'll hold a cocktail-party here in this very room and you and Betty and Bill shall come to it.'

The thought of Bill stabbed Martin's heart with the jealousy which he could not control inside him, although he gave no outward expression of it.

'I think you must let me give a party for you,' he said gently. 'Delia, aged twenty-one? It doesn't seem possible.'

'I feel like forty.'

'You still look such a child.'

'Appearances are deceptive, my dear Martin! But look here, it's half-past seven and you've got tickets for this show. You must go. Won't Mrs. Warnleigh go with you?'

He sighed.

'I'll ask her. But I wish you were coming — I was so looking forward to our evening.'

'So was I — 'but there's always tomorrow'!' She broke into the chorus of the popular song. 'Besides, I don't know what Mrs. Jenkins, my landlady, will say if I entertain young men in my bedroom.'

Martin smiled.

'It's a sitting-room as well, isn't it?'

'Oh yes, but so far I've had nobody here but Betty.'

'Betty's been a good friend.'

'She's been absolutely wonderful. When I think of Connie Berrell and some of the others who used to rush round me in the old days — ' Delia finished with a curl of her red lips and a shrug of her shoulders.

'Oh well,' sighed Martin. 'If I'm to be turfed out on a point of respectability, being a staid old lawyer, I'd better go.'

'You don't look staid, Martin.'

'I thought I did.'

'In the daytime — but when you get into a white tie and tails you look quite gay.'

'I don't feel gay having to leave you behind here.'

'Never mind — picture me going fast asleep about ten minutes after you go.'

He made no answer. The picture of

Delia curled up, sleeping in her bed was something he dared not contemplate.

If she had held out a hand and said: 'stay' he would have knelt down beside her and gathered her to his heart. But she said nothing. It wasn't Delia's way to make the first move. She smiled and waved a hand at him.

Had he been more experienced with women he might have known that a woman often says 'go' when she means 'stay'; might have guessed that she was unbearably lonely and tired of everything tonight; might have discovered depths in her ready and waiting to be explored. But he was a shy man, incurably reticent, and without conceit. He thought she wanted him to go and he left her without any knowledge of her receptive state of mind.

He would have been greatly astonished had he known that after he left her, Delia abandoned her cigarette, collapsed in a little heap on her bed and wept bitterly, although she would have found it hard to explain, even to herself, exactly why she cried.

There was a thunderstorm that night. Delia slept through it, undisturbed, so badly was she in need of rest. But in the morning she awakened to a leaden sky and pouring rain. The storm had put an end to the unseasonable heat. This was a real autumn day.

She was drenched to the skin when she got back to her room late that afternoon, but it had been a less tiring and depressing day than yesterday and the work seemed well worth while when she achieved even one sale.

When she reached home she saw a handsome Jaguar with a green body standing outside the house. Bill's car. He had bought it to use during his six months' leave. It was by now quite a familiar sight to Delia. She had had one or two very pleasant runs in the Jag and Bill let her drive, which she adored doing.

She wondered why he was here.

'I must look a fright,' she thought. 'But Bill will have to put up with it.'

Jenny appeared.

'Thumbs up!' she said, grinning all over her pasty little face. 'Captain Radleigh is 'ere to see you and the boss told me to put 'im into 'er parlour as she didn't think you'd wish to see 'im in your room, seein' as 'ow there's a bed in it.'

Delia collapsed weakly into laughter. Queer, how some people inevitably connected a bed with wickedness!

'Tell Captain Radleigh I'll be with him in a moment,' she said. 'I must just powder my nose.'

Jenny came close to her and whispered:

'No impudence meant, but I must say 'e isn't arf 'andsome! Jest like Richard Burton.'

'I'll tell him, Jenny,' said Delia. 'I'm sure he will be most flattered.'

Five minutes later she was greeting Bill in Mrs. Jenkins's dark parlour.

Bill's huge, athletic figure seemed to fill the little room. He looked immaculate as usual. He turned eagerly to

161

Delia when she entered.

'Ah, here you are!'

'My dear Bill, what are you doing in Mrs. Jenkins's parlour?'

'Admiring the wedding groups and the grandparents and grandchildren of Mrs. Jenkins,' said Bill with a humorous smile. 'You don't mind me coming, do you, Delia? It's been such a filthy day and I've been so bored — I felt I must have a look at you and find out if you'd like to come along and dance or do something cheery.'

'I've only just got back from work,' she told him.

He looked at her with the unmistakable light of a passionate admiration in his nice blue eyes.

'You look sweet!' he said.

Delia fluttered her lashes theatrically.

'Trust the Army to say the right thing. I'm pretty shabby. I've never looked worse.'

'For the first and only time in this life I disagree with you.'

'I don't suppose it will be the only

time, Bill. If we are to be friends we're certain to disagree now and then. It wouldn't be human not to!'

'H'm, well we haven't quarrelled yet. And I'm not starting tonight. I want to take you out.'

'But, Bill, we had an appointment for *tomorrow* night.'

'The more the merrier.'

'I'm sure you must have other things to do.'

'I've been doing them all day. Chose a new suit this morning; had my hair cut; met a maiden aunt for lunch. Now I want to enjoy myself.'

She laughed.

'You are absurd.'

'It was a lucky break for me, meeting you on the boat that day, Delia,' he said more seriously.

'Bill, you are a first-class flatterer.'

'No, I mean it. You don't know how I look forward to these evenings with you. It's made all the difference to my leave. You will come out, won't you?'

'I'm sure Mrs. Jenkins won't approve

of my going out two nights running with the same young man.'

'Blah!'

'And by the way,' added Delia, 'Jenny, our divine daily, thinks you ain't 'arf 'andsome and just like Richard Burton.'

Bill dropped into a chair in a mock faint.

'I can't survive that.'

'But he's most attractive.'

'Do *you* think so?'

'Jenny thinks so,' said Delia, then feeling that she was being a trifle coy, said hastily: 'I'll come out with you, Bill, if I can get into some evening shoes. I couldn't last night. I was so done in with the heat.'

He nodded.

'Carting round that damned awful sweeper, I suppose!'

'You and Martin are very unkind about my sweeper. It earns me my living. I made a couple of quid commission, today, selling one. I assure you, Captain Radleigh, if you just give our wonderful machine a test, you'll never use any other — '

He sprang to his feet and held up a warning hand.

'Stop! Even for you I won't be lured into buying an electric sweeper.'

She giggled.

'I was only practising my professional voice on you.'

'Go and get your pretty clothes on,' he begged, 'and come out to dinner.'

'I don't really feel that I ought to — even if I can get into my shoes.'

'Why not?'

'Well, I feel rather mean because I turned down Martin last night.'

'That doesn't mean to say you can't come out with me.'

'N-no,' she said in a hesitating voice.

'Get dressed — quickly — the aspidistra's depressing me,' he grinned.

The good humour and charm of the man were irresistible. Delia laughed and retired to her room, to have a speedy bath and change.

It was definitely good to scent the

bath water with her favourite salts and emerge from it refreshed and perfumed, then put on one of the beautiful lacy lingerie sets which she had bought in Paris, just before the crash came, and finally a very short silky dress of coral pink with beads round her throat to match. The pink shoes slid on quite easily tonight. No difficulty about that. A short coat completed a very chic outfit and when this vision presented itself to Bill, he gasped. She looked lovelier than he had ever seen her.

'I say! And is *this* our young commercial traveller?'

She gave a little laugh, opened her bag and found a cigarette.

'All that is left of the old wardrobe, Bill. I just kept two nice evening dresses — I sold all the rest.'

'It's a sin and a shame. You were meant to have lovely things — you're so lovely yourself.'

Her cheeks burned.

'Give me a match, Bill, and stop talking nonsense. You may be Burton but I'm *not* Liz Taylor.'

'Never seen the lady, but I'm sure you're better-looking.'

Delia's red under-lip stuck out rebelliously.

'Don't be so stupid!'

The man's brown, handsome face grew suddenly grave. He was on the verge of lighting her cigarette and then paused, the match in his hand.

He caught the slender fingers which were holding her cigarette and carried them to his lips.

'I may be stupid but I love you. I'm madly in love with you. It all started on the boat, crossing from Dieppe. Delia, we can't go on like this. You've got to marry me. Darling — darling, please — '

He broke off, stammering, the red blood burning through his tan. For a moment she was speechless, carried away on the tide of his fervour. She found herself in his arms. He was holding her so close to him that she could scarcely breathe, and buried his lips in her hair.

'Sweet thing, Delia! The sweetest, pluckiest girl I've ever met in my life. Delia — will you marry me? You've got to say 'yes' — you'll break me up if you say 'no'.'

'But, Bill — ' she began, feeling dizzy.

'You've got to say 'yes',' he interrupted. 'I adore you. There's never been anybody else — I mean there have been one or two affairs — but they've never meant anything. I always thought I'd be a bachelor — but I want to marry you — oh, *darling*!'

'But you know my — my position — ' she stammered.

'What do I care about that? I've got private means and my pay. I can't give you as much as you used to have — but I can make life more comfortable for you than it is now. And by God, I'll make it happier, too. I'll do anything to make you happy. But you can't go on working like this.'

'Yes, I can — ' she began weakly.

'You can't! I won't let you! I love you — love every bit of you. Marry me,

Delia, and come back with me out East in the spring.'

She tried to think, to analyse her feelings.

The memory of Lingo flashed through her mind. She had been prepared to face divorce, disgrace, quite a lot for Lingo's sake. That had been the first big thing in her life so far as sex was concerned. But did she care for Bill Radleigh as she had cared for Lingo? He was much nicer, much more dependable, much more sincere! But did he mean what Lingo had meant?

'For God's sake, say you'll marry me,' came Bill's almost agonised voice. 'It'll break my heart, honestly, if you turn me down. There isn't anybody else for you. I mean — is there?'

'Nobody,' she whispered.

There were no men in her life — except Bill — and Martin! And Martin was not in love with her. He was only sorry for her. Probably he would be pleased if she married a decent man like Bill.

She put away the thought of Martin. She felt suddenly that it was very sweet and thrilling to feel Bill's arms around her and listen to his wild protestations of love.

He looked down at her intently and saw that her breast was rising and falling quickly and that her eyes were wide and bright. She *was* a little stirred, then? Hope flamed through him.

'Marry me, Delia — dearest — please!'

She surrendered to the magic of the moment, curved a slim bare arm about his neck and tilted back her head.

'Do you really love me?'

'You know that.'

'Darling Bill! You've been so sweet to me — but the question is, do *I* love *you*?'

He tightened both arms about the charming young figure in the coral pink chiffon dress.

'You do — don't you — a little bit?'

'A little, yes,' she whispered. 'But I once loved somebody else — much more. I vowed I'd never care for anybody again.'

'That vow was meant to be broken — for me. You're going to love me much more than you loved him.'

'Oh, I don't know!' she sighed.

'Give it a chance — I won't fail you, Delia.'

'I'm sure of that,' she said, and the tears started to her eyes.

He brushed the wet lashes with his lips.

'Dear, sweet little Delia! You mustn't cry. Just tell me that you'll marry me and give me a chance to make you happy — and make you love me more than a little bit.'

'If you really want me — '

'Delia!' he exclaimed with a deep throb in his voice, and set his lips to her mouth.

When that long kiss, strangely satisfying to them both, came to an end, Delia found herself engaged to be married.

He walked on air during the rest of

that evening; boundless in his enthusiasm, white-hot with ardour. They had a celebration dinner at Malmaison. Bill was reckless — there were special flowers for her table — the best champagne — a perfect and specially ordered meal.

When she protested, he laughed and looked at her in that way which was beginning to intoxicate her a little.

'I only wish I were a millionaire — that I could buy up the whole of London for you to celebrate tonight. You don't know how much I love you. Nothing can be too good for you. And this night can never come again — so it's got to be a good one.'

He made her amazingly happy.

Before their little dinner ended, Delia was certain that she was not making a mistake. She wanted to marry Bill and to forget all the misery and bitterness of the last few months.

After dinner they went to a cinema. The Burtons were being featured at one of the West End houses and Delia insisted upon taking her newly-made fiancé to see them.

'You shall be introduced to your double — but you're not to get conceited. For Burton is really very good-looking.'

In the car, before driving to the pictures, Bill put an arm around her and, for a moment, Piccadilly and its lights and traffic and crowds faded out. Delia felt his hard lips against her mouth and closed her eyes under the sharp sweetness of that kiss. She felt that it would not be long before she was as much in love with this man as he was with her. His fervour was setting light to hers. And it seemed suddenly a wonderful thing that there was something to look forward to in the future. Marriage with a man like Bill — and — so he assured her — a gay, full life. She would be a huge success. His only fear was that she was too attractive, would be too much of a success. She laughed at that.

'You needn't have any anxieties. I

'shall be a faithful wife.'

'And a terribly attractive one,' he said huskily. 'God, Delia, you don't know how happy you've made me.'

'You've made me happy, too,' she said softly.

'There's no need for a long engagement. You'll marry me at once?'

She hesitated. She knew that she was going to be happy with this man and yet — that independent spirit of hers was shaken by the prospect of being entirely possessed by any man.

'Don't keep me waiting too long, honey,' he said, his arm still around her as they drove down Regent Street. 'Let's get married quickly and have a long honeymoon. We'll escape the bad weather — if it's going to set in. We'll go to the Riviera — Monte Carlo — Spain — anywhere you like. I'll get some currency.'

'I'd like to see Spain again,' she said wistfully. 'I motored through it with Daddy, and adored it.'

'Then marry me, and come to Spain

for a honeymoon,' he urged her.

She gave a breathless little laugh and moved away from his encircling arm.

'Perhaps I will — I'll think about it tonight and tell you tomorrow.'

His blue eyes looked suddenly horrified.

'You won't turn me down, now?'

She shook her head.

'No, I'll marry you, Bill. I've said so — I want to.'

'Angel!' He carried both her hands to his lips and covered them with kisses.

She looked down at the bent, brown head of the man.

'I wonder what Martin will say — '

Almost as though Bill read her thoughts, he said:

'We must tell your solicitor friend.'

'Yes — I'll ring Martin up tomorrow.'

'Will he approve of me? He's a sort of guardian to you, isn't he?'

'Not officially. But he has looked after me since Daddy died — he was Daddy's executor.'

'Good feller,' said Bill happily, and

did not give Martin Revell another thought that evening. He was much too intent upon persuading Delia to an early marriage.

But Delia thought about Martin at intervals and was annoyed with herself because his memory haunted her.

This engagement to Bill would, more or less, finish things with Martin, she knew. He would no longer manage her affairs. Bill would do that and in a few months' time Bill would take her abroad, and she would see little more of England or her friends in London except when they came home on leave. Army officers' wives were tied with their husbands for years at a stretch.

'You look sad, darling,' Bill said, with his lips close to her ear. 'Nothing worrying you, is it?'

'Nothing, Bill, but I've decided one thing. I'll marry you when you like.'

'Oh, my darling!' he said, and caught her close.

She clung to him suddenly, and lay with closed eyes against him while he caressed her. And she felt that an early marriage with Bill would be the best possible thing; put an end to all the difficulties. She would go right away with him and start a new life and find new happiness.

It was a full and exciting evening for Delia. Once they reached the cinema she stopped being introspective and allowed Bill to carry her with him blindly along the path of enchantment.

They ended up at Ciro's and danced till the early hours of the morning. And then when the car returned to Bayswater it stopped outside Mrs. Jenkins's lodging for longer than it takes to say a mere good-night.

'I can't let you go,' Bill kept saying. 'You're so sweet.'

Delia, thrilling to his caresses, had to be firm.

'I wouldn't mind taking the wheel and driving right round London,' she said. 'Only, first of all, it's a wet night and the roads are skiddy, and secondly we must be sensible.'

'I'll fetch you tomorrow morning and we'll go and choose the engagement ring.

Delia, pulling her coat close about her, prepared to step out of the car, but Bill lifted her firmly off her feet and planted her on the doorstep, kissing her as he did so. It was still drizzling and he would not allow her to get her shoes wet.

She grimaced at him.

'What a cave-man I've got myself engaged to.'

'You're so small, it will be easy to deal with you,' he said. 'I shall be your bearer out East and carry you about the bungalow.'

'I can't believe yet that I'm going to live abroad.'

'Well, you are, and what about this engagement ring?' he repeated.

'I've got to work tomorrow, my dear.'

'Oh, rot, I'm not going to have my future wife selling electric carpet-sweepers.'

'Now, don't be a snob, Bill.'

'It isn't a question of that. I've only got a certain amount of leave and I want to spend every hour of it with you. Besides, there's no need for you to work now.'

Out came Delia's red under-lip.

'This is where we have our first quarrel.'

'If it's going to be a long one, you'll catch cold — I'd better come in with you.'

'Certainly not! Mrs. Jenkins would throw a fit.'

'All right.' Bill took off his Burberry and wrapped it around the slim, pretty figure. 'Argue with me in that.'

'Bill, I must go on earning my living until we are married.'

'Why?'

'Don't be trying — I've got to make some money — for my trousseau — ' Her eyes sparkled at him mischievously.

He caught her hand.

'It's you who are being trying. Delia — I don't want you to go on with that job — please!'

'I must till I'm married,' she said obstinately.

'Then marry me by special licence tomorrow.'

'You great silly!'

'The day after tomorrow, then. You said you'd marry me when I wanted.'

'In a fortnight — no sooner.'

'If you insist.'

'And I'll throw up my job at the end of next week, if you like.'

With that he had to be content. Tomorrow was a Saturday. She promised to spend the afternoon and evening with him. He took a pearl ring she was wearing, as a pattern of size, and announced his intention of choosing something for her on approval in the morning and showing it to her when they met for lunch.

'What would you like?' he asked her. 'What is your favourite stone?'

'I don't think I have one. I hate modern diamonds — and I don't want anything expensive — I'll leave it to you.'

'Right! I shall get it at Woolworth's,' he said solemnly.

The dark, almond eyes sparkled at him. For a moment he caught her in his arms and held her close.

'Till tomorrow, angel.'

She walked into her bedroom yawning sleepily, and listened to the sound of the car going down the road until it died away into silence.

She looked at a leather case which lay on the floor in the corner of her room. Suddenly the red point of her tongue appeared impishly.

'Yah!' she said. 'Yah to you, my dear carpet-sweeper! One more week and then I need never exhibit your charms to anybody in this world again.'

That was certainly a relief. She flung up her arms with a little sigh and closed her eyes ecstatically.

Suddenly all feeling of fatigue left Delia. She felt that she could not sleep until she had written to Betty. Betty would be so glad, for her sake, that something like this had happened.

Betty liked Bill very much and, what was more, Betty liked John Blaker, Bill's adjutant friend who had been with them at the picnic a fortnight ago. Betty and Captain Blaker had met again since then — romance was in the air.

'It's good to be alive,' thought Delia, as she wrote to her friend.

The grey light of morning filtered through the curtains into her room before she finally drifted into sleep.

Martin was trying to reason with an elderly client who wished to float a new company on insufficient capital, when Delia rang him up, about eleven o'clock that next morning.

Martin's heart leaped.

'Yes, my dear?'

An excited little laugh reached him.

'I had to speak to you. I've gone quite mad. I'm supposed to be selling my carpet-sweeper but I'm in a tea-shop, having a bun and a cup of coffee, and phoning you.'

'What's happened?'

'Something rather wonderful.'

'What?' Martin's fingers gripped the telephone very tightly.

'I'm engaged to be married.'

'A thousand congratulations. I think I know the man, don't I?'

'Yes, it's Bill.'

Martin swallowed hard. Of course it was Bill.

'Delia, you will forgive me,' he said. 'I have a client here — I'd like to get in touch with you later. Will you lunch with me?'

'Can't. I'm lunching with Bill.'

'Just before lunch, then.'

'All right. I'll call at the office.'

Martin hung up the receiver. Everything was still rather dark before his vision, and his heart was beating at a violent and uncomfortable rate. Delia engaged . . . Delia about to be married . . . that would mean she would often go abroad, thousands of miles away, and he would hardly ever see her again. The idea was intolerable.

He bent over his desk.

The morning seemed to drag interminably, before the time came when Delia was due to call at the office.

Martin could not concentrate upon his work, could not think of anything or anybody but Delia and the fact that she was engaged and lost to him for ever.

At one o'clock Delia had not come. At half-past one she was still conspicuous by her absence. Martin, pacing up and down his room, glancing anxiously at his wrist-watch, began to think that she was not coming. But it was peculiar — unlike her to be so discourteous. Surely she had not gone to her appointment with Radleigh and forgotten about him, Martin?

At a quarter to two Martin decided that he would telephone through to Delia's lodgings. Mrs. Jenkins, the landlady, told him that Miss Beringham was in.

Martin began to feel a trifle resentful. If Delia was too occupied to call at the office, she might at least have let him know. He said a trifle curtly:

'Tell her that Mr. Revell wants to speak to her.'

'I'll tell her,' said Mrs. Jenkins's voice. 'But I doubt if she'll come, poor little soul.'

'Why?' demanded Martin. 'What's the matter?'

'She's 'ad terrible news,' said Mrs. Jenkins. ''Er friend, Miss Willis, and a gentleman is with 'er, now.'

That was enough for Martin. He hung up the receiver, picked up his hat and coat and hailed a taxi outside the office.

He could not for the life of him think what Delia's terrible news could be. Something to do with Radleigh, perhaps? But no, only a couple of hours ago she had told him, happily, of her engagement.

Whatever it was, Martin was going to her. If she was in some sort of trouble she might need him and his help.

Some two hours previously Delia, eating her bun and drinking her coffee in a Dulwich tea-shop, had felt thoroughly content. She had just spoken to Martin on the telephone. And she had just sold a sweeper. Her luck was in — just because she did not really care whether she sold one or not, she thought with cynicism. However, she did not despise the money. She needed it. She wanted to go to Bill with a really nice trousseau despite all his assurances that he would give her everything she wanted once they were married.

She had half hoped that he would telephone to her early this morning. It would be rather nice and thrilling to say a few words before she started on her rounds. But no message came. And Delia, picturing Bill fast asleep at Brown's Hotel, decided not to wake him up. She, on the other hand, had to make an early start in order to get through the number of houses on her list.

At twelve o'clock she made up her mind to 'chuck' work for today. It had been a triumph to get rid of one sweeper on a Saturday morning and there was nothing much doing now, before the week-end. She would go home, change her dress and make herself 'all nice and pretty' for her lunch with Bill. She intended to call at Martin's office on the way to her meeting with him.

At a quarter past twelve she reached her lodgings and saw a car outside which was not Bill's. Then suddenly she recognised it. It belonged to Captain Blaker, Bill's friend. She could not imagine why he should be calling here at this time of the day.

The front door was opened to her by Betty. Another surprise. But Delia hailed the tall, pretty girl with delight.

'How are you, Betts darling? You look lovely in that blue suit. Is it Fortnum?'

She paused, her smile fading. She saw Betty's face — grave and concerned. She added:

'What is it? Anything happened?'

'Yes, darling,' said Betty, in a low voice. 'I'm afraid so. Come in. Captain

Blaker's here, too. We came together.'

'But why?' asked Delia, now wholly astonished as she followed her friend into her bed-sitting-room. She found Captain Blaker standing in the middle of the room, smoking a cigarette. He was as a rule a cheerful man with a ready smile, but today he was the picture of gloom. He held out a hand to Delia, in silence, gripped her fingers tightly, then dropped them again and looked away.

Delia put her suitcase on the floor, took off her coat and beret and stared from Betty to the man.

'You are a grave pair!' she exclaimed. 'What in the world has gone wrong?'

Betty exchanged glances with Captain Blaker. The latter tugged uneasily at his collar.

'You'd better tell her,' he said gruffly, and moved over to the window and stood there with his back to them.

Betty, her large blue eyes filling with tears, put out an arm and put it around Delia's shoulders.

'Darling, we've been trying frantically to get you. We came round half an hour ago and Mrs. Jenkins told us you were out working and that you were lunching out, too. So we stayed here, hoping that you might come in to change before you met — '

She did not utter the name. But Delia said it.

'Bill — yes, I'm lunching with Bill.'

Dead silence. Betty threw a desperate look at the tall, soldierly figure of Blaker, but he did not turn round, so she went on, unaided, with her melancholy task.

'Delia darling, you must prepare yourself for a dreadful shock. Bill won't — won't be able to meet you for lunch.'

Then suddenly Delia seemed to realise that there was some very grave reason why John Blaker and Betty were here like this, this morning, and that the reason was connected with Bill. Something had happened to him. She caught her breath.

'Is he ill? What's the matter — tell me — ' she said in a frightened voice.

'I don't know how to tell you, darling.'

Delia gave her friend's hand a little shake.

'Of course you must tell me — is he ill?' she repeated.

'More than that, Delia.'

The hot colour flew to Delia's face and then receded. Her heart seemed to stand still.

'What do you mean? For goodness sake, go on — what *is* it?'

But Betty, sensitive and emotional, and not very good at standing up to a test like this, suddenly broke down and wept.

'John!' she appealed to Blaker. 'You tell her, please — I can't.'

Blaker turned round.

'I'm so terribly sorry to have to bring you such news, but you've got to know. Last night when poor old Bill left you, that car of his skidded — you know how wet it was — and the roads were greasy — '

He broke off with a little gesture of

the hand. Delia, her bright dark eyes fixed upon him, nodded.

'I know — I noticed they were greasy — I warned Bill to be careful when he was driving me home. He's had an accident?'

'Yes, he skidded into a mail van, and there was an awful crash.'

Delia's delicate nostrils dilated.

'What's happened — please tell me everything.'

'The car got the worst of it. Poor old Bill was badly knocked about — hit his head. He was taken to hospital. There was nothing on him, apparently, to give them any idea who he was, and he did not recover consciousness until this morning. Then he sent for me. We'd been close friends for years. And he hadn't any relative he particularly cared about — '

The colour burned Delia's cheeks again. Her hands were shaking.

'He had — me! Why didn't he send for me? I must go to him now — of course — '

'One moment,' said Blaker gently, and laid a kind hand on her shoulder. 'It's a bit worse than you think. You see, Bill knew that he was not going to last out when he sent for me. He didn't want to harrow you — as I told you, he was rather smashed up, poor old chap. And he wanted you to remember him as he was. He told me that you two had fixed it up to get married last night. It's an absolute tragedy — for both of you — '

Blaker broke off huskily and turned his face away.

A low cry came from Delia.

'Captain Blaker — Bill isn't — *dead*?'

'I'm afraid he is. He became unconscious again after I left him and never recovered. I was at my club — and I asked them to ring me and tell me, and they did. Then I got hold of Miss Willis — Betty — and we both came round here to you. I was devoted to Bill, myself; it's an awful loss for me as well as for you. His last message to you was to carry on and not grieve for him and just try to remember what happiness you had together.'

Delia stood very still. There was not a vestige of colour in her face now, and her eyes were wide and horrified.

She said, slowly and with difficulty:

'I wrote to you, Betty, when I got back from my evening out with Bill. You'll get the letter some time this morning.'

Betty shook her head, weeping bitterly. But Delia did not weep. Dry-eyed, and with her new world of happiness crashing in ruins around her, she questioned Blaker.

'Was he — very badly hurt?'

'Yes, but he did not suffer. His spine was injured.'

'I'm so glad of that,' she whispered. 'I shouldn't like Bill to have suffered.'

'He was hardly ever conscious except when he spoke to me. They said he had a very peaceful end.'

'I wish I had — been there — just to help him.'

'He might not even have recognised

you,' said Blaker, with a compassionate look at her. 'And he was so keen that you should not be harrowed by a death-bed scene.'

'It was like him to be so — thoughtful.'

'He sent you all his love and — this.'

Blaker, wishing somehow that this slim, dark-eyed girl were not quite so brave, so gallant, pulled a ring out of his pocket and handed it to her.

'Bill's signet ring. He'd like you to keep it.'

Delia took the ring. Her fingers closed over it convulsively. She said:

'Thank you so much. I'm glad to have that.'

'I've wired to his aunt, Miss Radleigh, who lives down in Gloucestershire, and that's all that I can do.'

'I'd like to get in touch with her,' said Delia tonelessly.

'Oh, and poor old Bill sent you another message.'

'Yes?'

'He asked that you shouldn't go to

his funeral, or have anything to do with that business of flowers or mourning. He was so anxious you should remember nothing but your cheery times together. He wanted you to try and feel that he had passed like a dream.'

That shook even Delia's courage. She said in an anguished voice:

'Thank you — for everything — now please — do you mind going away and leaving me alone? I'd love to see you — both — some other time, but not now.'

Betty embraced her.

'Send for me when you want me, darling.'

'Thank you, Betty.'

'Sure you wouldn't like me to stay now?'

'No — I just want to — be alone.'

Blaker shook Delia's hand.

'I'll see you again,' he said. 'And you know, without me telling you, how terribly sorry I am — '

'I am for you, too,' she whispered. 'He was such a wonderful friend — '

She turned away from him because the tears had come and were pouring down her cheeks.

John Blaker put on his hat, took Betty's arm, and led her out to his car.

'Come and lunch with me, Betty — you need a brandy-and-soda and I know I could do with one. God, what a tragedy! In the prime of his life — and just when she'd got fond of him. Poor child — a bit hard on her, and she's such a stoic!'

'More than a bit. And she's already had one tragedy with a man who let her down. She seems doomed.'

'I must say I take off my hat to her,' said Blaker, when they were in his car. 'She's one of the nicest girls I've ever met — except you — and she told me the other day what a brick you've been to her, through all her troubles.'

Betty's heart was too full for speech, but she moved, instinctively, a little nearer John Blaker. In a short time his hand came out and took hers, and they felt suddenly very close in mind as well as body.

Delia lay on her bed with her face pressed to the pillow. Bill's signet ring was still between her clenched fingers. She whispered:

'Oh, Bill — oh, *Bill*!'

When Martin arrived, hot-foot from his office, Delia had got back her self-control. Her eyes were red-rimmed with crying, but there were no more tears to be shed. The cherry-red lips were pressed tightly together and the small dark head held high.

'I'm glad you've come, Martin,' was her greeting to him.

He looked at her with concern, walked across her room and took both her hands.

'My dear, what is it? I phoned you when you didn't turn up at the office and Mrs. Jenkins said you'd had bad news and that Betty and some man were here with you.'

'They've only just gone.'

'Where's Radleigh? You were meeting

him for lunch — '

Delia thrust her hands into the pockets of her suit.

'He's — dead, Martin.'

Martin's heart missed a beat.

'*Dead!*' he repeated incredulously. 'Good God!'

'He was smashed up in the Jag after he left me last night. He died this morning in St. George's Hospital.'

'Good God!' repeated Martin, and stood flabbergasted while Delia told him all that John Blaker had imparted to her. Her eyes were fiercely bright but her red lips were trembling as she added:

'It's rotten luck — just when we'd made up our minds to get married — isn't it?'

'It's frightful!' said Martin. 'The most awful thing I've ever heard. Poor old Radleigh! Poor chap.'

'Yes, I resent it for his sake — he was so fond of life.'

Martin looked at her speechlessly. Her news had shocked him to the core.

And the sight of her white, set young face and the knowledge that she was still undaunted, pulled at his very heartstrings. He saw that she was suffering badly under that calm exterior. At last he found words.

'I really don't know what to say to you, it's all too ghastly — I'm more sorry than I can say.'

She tossed back a dark lock of hair with a characteristic gesture.

'It was his particular wish that I shouldn't go to his funeral or mourn for him — I shall just carry on with my work and try not to think about it.'

'But you can't go on with that rotten job.'

'I can, and I must,' she broke in. 'I've got to work — there isn't anything else ahead of me — now! Bill and I had made some wonderful plans but they're not going to materialise and I've got to face it, that's all.'

'My dear!' said Martin, helplessly.

'Of course it was a very short engagement — just a few hours,' said

Delia with an unhappy laugh.

'That doesn't say you weren't fond of him,' said Martin without a vestige of jealousy.

'I was. Very fond. And I think in time I would have got fonder. He was terrific.'

'My poor Delia.'

She tossed back her hair again.

'That's what life does to me — I'm just doomed not to be happy that way!'

He shook his head. He had no answer for her, only immeasurable pity which flooded his whole being and made him ache to comfort her.

She met his gaze and saw that thin, clever face of his convulsed. Blindly, she thrust out her hands to him.

'Don't be so sorry for me, Martin. I'm all right — I can stick it. You needn't worry.'

He caught the small hands and clung on to them as though it were he who needed her help more than she wanted his.

'Darling,' he said, unconsciously

using that endearment for the first time in their lives. 'I'd give anything in the world to bring Radleigh back — to give you back your happiness.'

Now the tears came stinging her eyelids again. Her fingers curled about his. She whispered:

'But you can't — that's the worst of life — it deals that sort of blow! . . . takes something away that one can never get back.'

'What can I do to help you?'

'Nothing — just go on being my friend. I really don't think I could bear it if I lost you now.'

'You won't lose me, darling child. Now, look here, you generally argue with me, but today I'm going to ask you to let me have my own way.'

'Thank you, Martin. What do you want me to do?'

'Come back to Hampstead with me for the week-end. Elinor's away — she's gone to stay with cousins in Sussex. Come and let Aunt Eva and me look after you, and if you insist on going

back to that wretched job on Monday
— well then you must go.'

She surrendered. She was too sore at
heart to offer any resistance. Besides,
she would rather be with Martin than
anybody, because he understood her so
well.

She packed a bag and allowed him
to take her back to Hampstead. When
she was in the car she suddenly
remembered John Blaker's story of
the car skidding ... Bill being
smashed up and taken by ambulance,
broken and dying, to the hospital.
Her imagination was vivid and she
gave a little gasp and suddenly clung
to Martin's hand and pressed her
eyes to his shoulder. He, guessing
what lay in her mind, told the driver
to go slowly. They went at a gentle
pace from Bayswater to Hampstead
— Martin with an arm about her
shoulders, she with her face hidden
against his sleeve.

★　★　★

A mild June morning, some nine months later, found Delia eating her breakfast in the bed-sitting-room in Bayswater holding a cup of tea in one hand and a *Morning Post* in the other. She was reading one paragraph in the *Post* which gave her evident enjoyment.

'*The engagement is announced between Captain John Arthur Blaker, youngest son of the late Colonel Arthur Blaker, and Mrs. Blaker of The Oaks, Stopford, Glos., and Elizabeth (Betty) Mary Willis of South Parks Mansions, Kensington. The marriage will take place in Hong Kong early in August.*'

With a little sigh Delia laid the paper down, finished her breakfast and hurriedly put on her hat. She would be late for work this morning, unless she rushed. As she pulled a small straw hat over her smooth dark head she thought: 'I'm so glad it's happened — I knew it would! Dear old Betty — I do hope she'll be happy — she ought to be, because John is a pet!'

She had known, of course, for months that Betty and John Blaker would end up like this. The romance, which had started in Bill's lifetime, had ripened slowly but surely after his death.

Now it was all settled. Betty was in the seventh heaven of delight and John was sending rapturous and expensive cables from Hong Kong. Betty, who had spent yesterday evening with Delia, had only one regret, she said — that her best and dearest friend could not be present at her wedding. But of course it was out of the question.

'No life with the Guards for me, my dear,' Delia told Betty. 'I'm one of the world's workers!'

That was not an unreasonable description of Delia, these days. She was working very hard. As soon as she had recovered from that first, sharp shock of losing Bill, after so brief an engagement, she had thrown herself, body and heart, into her job. No matter how uncongenial, work seemed the best antidote for mental suffering. Bill had asked her not to grieve for him and she tried to do as he wished. She locked his signet ring away in her jewel-case with the treasures which had belonged to her mother, and after that week-end at Hampstead with Martin and his aunt, never referred to the tragedy. Only Martin, who knew her well, was aware that she had not forgotten . . . that she was the type who would never forget.

The wound opened a little under the pressure of Betty's rhapsodies about John, just before he went away, and her forthcoming life in the Army. Betty was going to have all that she, Delia, had lost. But even Betty did not know quite how hard Delia had to fight her melancholy.

However, Delia was very young and she had not known or cared for Bill long enough for the thing to be a lasting tragedy. By now she was herself again and Bill could be remembered and spoken of normally once more.

Martin Revell was very much to the fore in Delia's life at the moment. His kindness and understanding after Bill's tragic accident left an indelible impression upon her. She felt that she could never be sufficiently grateful to him. He was unfailing in his attentions, his efforts to make things easier. He let her do what she wanted — no longer argued or worried her. He had learnt that Delia must go her own way and fight her own battles.

They had had some quite amusing evenings together lately. To please her he had learnt to dance, a thing which he had never before cared about. He was naturally light on his feet and of graceful build, and he danced very well indeed. He began to like it merely because he danced with her, although he did not tell her so. But she knew that he enjoyed himself. She had told him, jokingly, when they last met, that she thought she was having a bad influence on the staid lawyer.

'You hardly ever used to smile in the old days, Martin,' she said. 'But now you're quite different.'

'I should call it your good influence,' he had smiled back at her. 'I feel years younger.'

'It suits you,' she said. 'You're really very good-looking!'

Her light, jesting praise had made him blush like a boy but he had found an equally light answer for her. She had taught him that it was wise not to take himself too seriously.

She had spent Christmas with him and Mrs. Warnleigh had been touched and gratified by their kindness to her. Even Elinor was amiable, Elinor who had once been bitterly jealous of the girl who occupied so much of Martin's time and thought.

But that had been sex jealousy and it had died when, during the autumn, romance entered Elinor's life. She had given up her hopeless dream about Martin. A certain young clergyman, with whom she had worked amongst the poor in the north of London, had offered her his heart and name and she had accepted.

They had been married since January and were shortly going to East Africa where Elinor's husband had taken a living. Delia had always thought that Elinor would end up by leading some kind of sacrificial life. Her devotion to Martin had been the result of her daily contact with him, but the arrival of her devoted clergyman had speedily put an end to her sorrows, and she was now in her true 'milieu'.

In the New Year Delia left the carpet-sweeper company. Trade was not good and Mr. Brown, acting on instructions from headquarters, had to cut down his travellers' list by half. Delia, none too well after a bad dose of flu, had not sold a sufficient number of sweepers recently to justify her existence in the firm, so she was one of the first to go.

A difficult and anxious month followed.

Then an old friend came to the rescue. In former days, Delia had known a rather famous Society beauty, by name Babs St. James. Babs married a man in the R.A.F. who proceeded to leave her soon after their marriage, for an actress. In the February of this year the beautiful Babs started a shop for hats and gowns. Society flocked to it and it was a big success. Betty, ever on the look-out for her friend, went to Babs for her clothes, and asked her to give Delia a job. There was a vacancy for a *vendeuse* and Delia stepped into it.

It was a more congenial job than that of selling carpet-sweepers, and better paid. It was also better for Delia's health; less tiring than that daily tramp from house to house in any kind of weather.

Babs's shop, which went by the name of 'Babette', was growing fast. She had a big showroom in Albemarle Street, and Delia was there from nine in the morning until six at night. She found it hard work standing all day, and coaxing difficult customers to buy, but it amused her and she liked it.

She had one horrible moment when Lingo Hewes walked into the shop with a girl who, she afterwards learned, was his latest infatuation, although he was still leading a cat and dog existence with Phil, his wife.

Lingo and Delia came face to face. He, as insolent as ever, greeted her with enthusiasm. But she had great pleasure in giving him her iciest smile, turned her attention to the platinum blonde who was his companion and charged him very much more than he need have paid for the hat which he was made to buy.

She was pleased to find how little it affected her to see Lingo again. She repeated the incident to Martin, with whom she dined that same night, and made him laugh at her description of Lingo's face when he wrote the cheque for what Delia called: 'Half a yard of felt and a feather.'

Delia was doomed to be late at 'Babette' this June morning because the telephone bell rang just as she was going out. Jenny rushed after her.

'It's for you, miss.'

Delia went back to the telephone. Martin's voice came over the wire.

'I want to see you this evening without fail — it's important.'

'My dear, how important — because I've fixed up to dine with one of the girls at the shop — '

'Put her off, there's a dear,' said Martin.

'Anything wrong?'

'N-no,' he said in a hesitating voice. 'Except that I've got to go away and I want to see you and tell you about it.'

'Go away where — when?'

'End of the week. To Spain.'

'Oh, Martin, not my beloved Spain?'

'Yes, on business, to Madrid. We have rather an important client there.'

She suddenly realised that she did not want Martin to go away. She saw him three or four times a week and without him London would seem flat. She said:

'I'll put my appointment off and meet you.'

'Nice child. Say seven-thirty, then, at Quaglino's.'

'Good-bye,' she said.

'Wait, Delia. On second thoughts, I'll come and fetch you. I'll bring my own car.'

She was nearly ready for him when he came that night, at a quarter past seven.

Martin gave one yearning look at her, then greeted her casually.

'You look well, tonight. You've got back your pink cheeks, Delia. Working at Babette's doesn't seem to do you any harm.'

'I like it,' said Delia cheerfully, and added: 'Now tell me your news.'

He lit a cigarette and watched her while she slipped into a short green velvet coat and pulled it deftly about her.

'As I told you, I'm going to Madrid

at the end of the week on important business.'

'How long will you be away?'

'A fortnight. This man has asked me to stay till the end of the month and combine business with pleasure. He wants me to go to the South — he has a villa there.'

Delia leant near her mirror and touched her lips with rouge. Her bright dark eyes glanced at the reflection of Martin. She said:

'Aren't you lucky!'

'I don't really want to go, but Aunt Eva's bullying me — says I need a holiday.'

'So you do. You haven't had one for months.'

'What about you, my child?'

'Oh, I can't afford one.'

Then she turned to him and gave a rather wistful smile.

'Can't you get your client to include me in the invitation — I'll come as your secretary. I can speak a little Spanish.'

He answered her lightly:

'You wouldn't come if I arranged it.'
Her eyes widened at him.

'But I would come — of *course* I would!' She came up to him and clutched his arms. 'Martin, you couldn't get your client to issue an invitation to a secretary, *could* you?'

She was so close that a drift of her hair touched his chin and he could smell the dear, familiar perfume which he associated with her. Suddenly the disaster, which he had been fearing and fighting, occurred. He lost control, took her hands, and flung them rudely away.

'You don't know what you're saying — don't be so damn silly — how could you possibly go to Madrid as my secretary? You talk about travelling abroad with a man as though he were — you were — ' He broke off, stammering, incoherent.

Delia, astounded, stared up at him. Her cheeks grew scarlet and her heart began to beat at an uncomfortable rate.

'I'm sorry, Martin,' she said slowly. 'I didn't mean to upset you.'

'No, but you do,' he said between his teeth.

'But why shouldn't I go with you as a secretary?' she asked in a grieved voice.

His passion broke bonds again.

'Because, you little fool, you're not the sort of girl a man could travel with platonically — at least I know *I* couldn't answer for myself with you. You're *not* Miss Pintoe — you're Delia Beringham — and I love you — I'm terribly in love with you and I have been for the hell of a long time — oh *God*, now I've done the one thing I didn't want to do!'

He dropped into a chair, pulled out a handkerchief and wiped his forehead. Delia stood in the centre of the room, her gaze fixed on him, her heart beating quicker than ever.

For a moment she neither moved nor spoke. She just went on looking at him; trying to absorb the real meaning of it all. Once, nearly a year ago, she had thought that she had seen into Martin's heart — had thought that he cared for her and that was why he had behaved so extraordinarily about Lingo. Now she knew that she had not been wrong. And she saw, too, the beautiful selflessness of Martin's behaviour to her after Bill Radleigh's death. His was real love, the love that eliminated self. She felt suddenly awed. She was not worth such a love. And she could not understand why Martin had singled her out as the object of his devotion.

Martin raised his head, put away his handkerchief, and met her gaze. His face was pale and gloomy.

'Sorry, Delia — I've made a fool of myself.'

She swallowed hard and walked slowly towards him.

'No,' she said. 'You haven't done that. If anybody's a fool — I am.'

I shouldn't have said what I did!

'I don't quite see why — '

'Because as long as you didn't know that I was in love with you, our friendship could go on. Now it can't.'

'Why, Martin?' she said.

'You ought to understand,' he said almost roughly. 'I told you just now you're not the sort of girl that a man can take to Madrid as his secretary. If I took you to Spain it would have to be as my wife or nothing, and I can't go on seeing you — just as a friend. I can't stand it.

'Don't you see,' went on Martin desperately. 'I've spoilt everything — and we'd better not meet any more after this evening.'

'Not meet any more — you and I — ' she said, aghast.

He drew a sharp sigh.

'You mean so much to me, Delia! I can't bear the idea of letting you go out of my life, but I suppose I've got to.'

She did not pause to think too deeply — she just acted then as instinct and impulse led her.

'But supposing I couldn't bear the idea of letting *you* go out of *my* life!' she said wildly.

'You can't mean that.'

'But, Martin, I do. After all we've

been through together — I *couldn't* say good-bye to you tonight, and never see you again.'

He caught both her hands and clung to them like a drowning man.

'Delia!'

She thrilled to the passion in his eyes and the convulsive clasp of his thin, nervous fingers. She stammered:

'If you won't take me to Madrid as an unmarried girl — then take me — *as your wife*! There, now, I've proposed to *you*, Martin. When you asked me to marry you after Daddy died, I thought you did it out of chivalry. But my proposal isn't at all chivalrous — it's just selfish — I'm terribly, terribly fond of you, Martin, and I don't want you to go away without me!'

'Oh, my dear!' he said, and took her in his arms and held her so close that she could feel the shaking of his heart-beats against her breast. 'Oh, my dear, I didn't ask you to marry me out of chivalry. I loved you. I've always loved you — but it always seemed so impossible, we were such miles apart in those days. Then there was Hewes, and then poor Radleigh — I had to keep in the background. I never thought it possible you might get fond of me.'

'I've always been fond of you, Martin, but it's only lately that I've known that I was more than fond.'

'Delia — darling — *darling* — are you sure you mean it?'

'Yes,' she whispered, and curved an arm about his neck and drew his head down to hers. 'I mean every word of it. There have been two men in my life — as you know. But looking back on everything I realise how much, much more deeply I love you than I've loved anybody else in the world.'

Martin shut his eyes.

'Sweet, I can't believe it — it is too fabulous to be true.'

'Are you sure you want me?' she whispered, and now there were tears in her eyes. 'I couldn't bear *this* to be another tragedy.'

'It will only be a tragedy,' he said, 'if

you changed your mind between now and tomorrow morning when I intend to book your passage with mine — for Madrid!'

'I shan't change, darling Martin,' she said between laughter and tears.

'My love,' he said huskily. 'It's been a dream of mine for days and nights and weeks and months. But now it's got to be reality!'

'It is,' she said, and raised her lips for his kiss.

LOVING LADY SARAH

J. Darley

As life returns to normal after the war, Lady Sarah Trenton's reality is put into perspective. Her love for Robert, the gamekeeper's son who has returned home safely, is as alive as ever. But they must meet in secret, for Lord Trenton, whose heart has been hardened by the loss of his son, intends to see his daughter marry a man of wealth and status — like the odious Sir Percy. The times are changing, but the class divide is as wide as ever. Will Sarah and Robert be forced apart?

FORBIDDEN FLOWERS

Alice Elliott

An embarrassing slip in the Hyde Park mud leads Lily and Rose Banister into the path of Philip Montgomery, a British Embassy diplomat. Mesmerised by Lily's beauty, he invites her to accompany him to the Paris Exhibition, while Rose, who can't help but feel envious, is asked to chaperone the trip. Arriving in Paris, the trio happen upon Philip's old adversary Gordon Pomfret, who decides to join their group, obviously vying for Lily's attention. Meanwhile, Rose and Philip discover that their shared interests might just make them kindred spirits . . .

CLOSE TO THE EDGE

Sheila Spencer-Smith

Grieving the death of her brother, Alix decides to make a fresh start on the Dorset coast. Her new job, running the tearoom attached to Mellstone Gallery, comes with its own difficulties — not least the petulant attitude of her employer's daughter Saskia. On top of this, Alix soon discovers the feud between her landlady and her neighbours, twins Cameron and Grant. Despite being warned to stay away, Alix is drawn to Cameron's warm nature. With his plans to move north and her turbulent past, could they have a future together?

SILENCED WITNESS

Tracey Walsh

Morven Jennings is a super recogniser: she has the ability to remember the faces of almost everyone she's ever seen. Having lived under an assumed identity in witness protection since the murder of her parents when she was sixteen, she hopes one day to spot the face of the killer in a CCTV image. But when her investigation of the abduction of a baby from Heathrow Airport takes her down unexpected avenues, it brings shadows of her past to light — and puts her in the sights of dangerous enemies . . .